I0520403

MICHELANGELO DICAPRIO

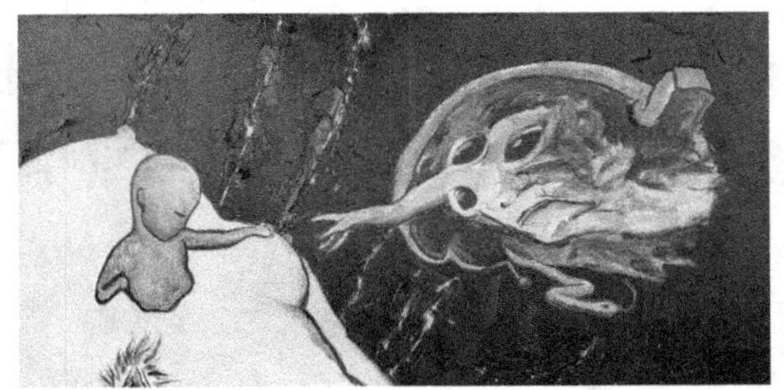

MARK HARRIS

LOSGET
Losget Press

2021

Disclaimer

THIS IS A NOVEL IN WHICH NOTHING IS TRUE, AND THE VIEWS OF ANY CHARACTER DO NOT REPRESENT THE AUTHOR'S VIEWS. ANY IDENTICAL OR SIMILAR CONTENT TO REAL NAMES, PERSONS (ALIVE OR DEAD), PLACES, OR EVENTS ARE PURELY COINCIDENTAL.

IT IS NOT RECOMMENDED TO IMITATE ANY FICTIONALLY DANGEROUS OR POTENTIALLY DANGEROUS BEHAVIOR IN THE NOVEL IN REAL LIFE.

Volume 1

THE BEST ACTOR

Author: Mark Harris
Painted and photographed by Mark Harris
Editor: Ellen Bitterman

Author: Mark Harris
Painted and photographed by Mark Harris
Editor: Ellen Bitterman
Author portrait by Chaoyang Lin

Published in the United States by Losget Press, Los Angeles.
Originally published in paperback in the United States by Losget Press, in 2021.
Library of Congress Cataloging-in-Publication Data
Names: Harris, Mark, author.
Title: Michelangelo DiCaprio: The Best Actor/ Mark Harris.
Description: First edition. | Los Angeles: Losget Press, 2021.
Identifiers: LCCN: 2020923991 | ISBN-13: 978-1-951364-10-6 | ISBN-10: 1-951364-10-4 | Ebook ISBN-13: 978-1-951364-06-9 | Ebook ISBN-10: 1-951364-06-6
Book design by Mark Harris, adapted for ebook
Cover design: Mark Harris
www.losget.com
E-mail: contact@losget.com
First printing. 2021.

Synopsis

Readers will enjoy the fantasy journey of the protagonist, Michelangelo DiCaprio, as he ventures forth to find a new life beyond the Great Wall that divides the United States and California. In this unique work of magical realism, *Michelangelo DiCaprio: The Best Actor*, author Mark Harris captivates readers with his use of humor, irony, and play on words to ultimately create a fictitious, yet strangely familiar world in which society's norms are upended. The novel takes readers on the protagonist's journey from the United States, a country depicted as underdeveloped and in deep decline and social disrepair, into the mythical world of a burgeoning and culturally lush California, which is no longer a part of the United States but rather a country unto itself.

As with any life quest, Michelangelo's travels are fraught with danger and confusion. He must overcome many obstacles that attempt to overpower him and even threaten to take his life. Ultimately, Michelangelo is forced by a mysterious phantom to become an actor and to fight for the coveted A-Star Award for Best Actor given only to Hollywood's most accomplished actors. Our protagonist has the opportunity to play the most prized role of all – that of God, himself. Will his quest for greatness succeed through his dogged determination or will he succumb to more powerful forces that seek to destroy him and his surroundings?

Author Mark Harris renders a brilliant story of an imagined world in which the protagonist is deeply challenged by his desires and emotions as he negotiates a world of high tech beyond his experience or understanding. The author intrigues readers with his ingenious references to many familiar aspects of traditional culture, such as the graphic design on the US dollar and Michelangelo's famous painting. Using a unique style of prose that will entertain and delight readers, Harris redefines the familiar and replaces it with an exciting and humorous new paradigm. *Michelangelo DiCaprio: The Best Actor* is an invitation to escape the confines of realism and cross over the Great Wall, along with the protagonist, into the imagined world of the author's creation. Michelangelo believes a better life awaits him in California, but his journey threatens to end in great destruction.

This novel will provide you with an exciting reading experience. Readers' perceptions of the world as they know it will be delightfully overturned as the author, with bold imagination, presents the United States as a backward country, California as a developing country, and Mexico as a developed country. You will break from reality and travel into a new reality of time and place. When you close this book and return to your everyday life, you will find that the real world is somehow new.

Mark Harris in 2015

Contents

The truth is that
Their two so-called eyes
Are just the locks
Of their real eyes.

CHAPTER 1

THE SUBWAY

Early morning in New York City in 1981, 7-year-old Michelangelo DiCaprio was asleep, held in his mother's arms as they entered the Grand Central–42nd Street subway station. Michelangelo's mother was a beautiful woman; she used to work in Studio 54; her name there was Disco Layla.

On the platform, Michelangelo woke up in his mom's arms. Some people were waiting for the train. A man with a pipe in his mouth was painting a mural. A man was lounging in a bathtub and smoking a Marlboro. A woman and a man were watering a small cornfield. Several disheveled young men were singing and playing—the singing one wore a pair of cut-off yellow trousers and his red vest was rolled up to his chest; the guy playing the guitar looked like his white vest had been torn in half.

"Mom, were they robbed?" Michelangelo broke free from his mom's arms.

"Probably. The security in the subway is terrible," mom said.

Just then, a train roared in. The dilapidated train was pulled by rows of giant mice as big as donkeys, followed by the mischief of little mice chattering. The driver sitting at the front part of the train tugged at the reins so hard that the rows of giant mice screamed. The train stopped fiercely in front of the people waiting for it. The little mice scattered. Michelangelo followed his mom into a subway car.

The driver squeezed a cat in his arms, and the cat uttered a scream. The rows of giant mice screamed in terror and ran the train. The little mice ran after the train excitedly.

—

In this subway car, several people crowded into a long seat and gathered in front of a "TV set." They shouted out excitedly and repeatedly.

"How can they take up seats!" Michelangelo whispered to his mom. It made them feel bad to imagine telling the guys that the monochrome screen gadget was not a TV set. However, Michelangelo and his mom could not bear to watch the guys waste their life, so they went to the next car.

In this car, several police were burning books; smoke filled the car. Mom hurriedly covered Michelangelo's nose and mouth; however, he could still ask the police, "Hasn't TV encouraged us to read more books? Why are you burning them?"

"It also said on TV that the man who shot Mr. Lennon was keen to read, kiddo," a policeman replied.

"Why would reading make people kill others?" Michelangelo asked.

"It's only an individual case; it doesn't mean anything. But I think that reading too much will indeed make you stupid, so I am happy to burn these books," said the policeman.

Mom was angry at the policeman's answer and took Michelangelo to the next car.

—

In this car, the long seat on one side was full of people. Michelangelo recognized that the older man in the middle was the newly elected President. He tugged on his mom excitedly; she looked a little nervous and kept smoothing her long hair.

On the long seat on the other side, a man sat down reading a book. Mom led Michelangelo to sit next to him. Michelangelo was a little scared of the man because of what the policeman had said.

The President smiled kindly at Michelangelo and took out a mouse doll. Mom hurriedly pulled Michelangelo to his feet. Michelangelo happily accepted the gift after bowing to the President. The President touched his hair affectionately.

"Mr. President, is it fun to be a president?" Michelangelo asked.

"It's not fun and one can die at any time,"

the President replied.

"Then why do you continue to be president?" Michelangelo asked.

"Make America Great Again!" the President replied.

"Did you want to be president since you were a kid?" Michelangelo asked.

"No, I used to be a film actor, and that was my dream when I was a kid," the President replied.

"Then why haven't I seen your films?" Michelangelo asked.

"I was not very successful as an actor," the President replied.

"Then you became president because you were unsuccessful as an actor?" Michelangelo kept asking.

"Michelangelo, you can't talk to Mr. President like this; it is impolite," his mom said.

"It's ok; it's a good question. Frankly speaking, being an actor is indeed a bit difficult for me," the President answered.

"I see! Being an actor is more awesome than being a president. I want to be an actor when I grow up," Michelangelo said.

After returning to his seat, Michelangelo

excitedly played with the mouse doll. Michelangelo's mother whispered to the man sitting next to her, "I heard that reading too much may cause stupidity."

"Ma'am, you shouldn't be so rude," the man said. "Jodie is studying literature at Yale University. She is the most beautiful and intelligent woman in the world."

"Oh, I happen to be one of Jodie's fans." Michelangelo's mother was a little embarrassed. "Then she must be pleased to know you love to read."

"No, she doesn't know it. You can't get love from reading." With that, the man pulled out a pistol and shot the President many times.

Several men around the President were hit and fell while protecting him. The man pointed the smoking gun at the President's head. Michelangelo's mother kicked him with her high heel. "You scared my son!"

The kick caused the man's bullet to miss. Although the President was injured, it was better than a shot to the head. The uninjured men knocked the man down. The shocked mother hurriedly dragged Michelangelo to the next car.

—

Only a woman and a little girl were in this car; they were a mother and daughter. Michelangelo's mother took him to sit opposite them and they smiled and nodded at each other.

The little girl looked a little younger than Michelangelo. She seemed to like Michelangelo very much and kept staring at him and smiling. Michelangelo's mother encouraged him to greet her.

"Hello, my name is Michelangelo Di-Caprio. This mouse doll was a gift from Mr. President," Michelangelo said to the little girl.

"Hello, my name is Elizabeth. May I touch it?" The little girl had a British accent.

"My pleasure." Michelangelo walked over and handed the mouse doll to her. Instead of taking the mouse doll, she just touched it admiringly.

"Are you from Britain? Do you like New York?" Michelangelo asked.

"Yes, I'm from Reading. I kind of like New

York now because I like this mouse doll," Elizabeth replied with a smile.

"What? What do you mean by 'reading'?" Michelangelo asked.

"Yes, Reading; it's my hometown in Berkshire, South East England," Elizabeth answered.

"Amazing! There must be many books in your hometown." Michelangelo tugged at his mother. "Mom, may I gift the mouse doll to my Reading friend?"

"That's great!" she said. "I'm sure Mr. President will be glad about that."

"Elizabeth, may I gift you this mouse doll?" Michelangelo asked.

"But...but I don't have a gift back for you." Elizabeth took a peek at her mother with a little bit of loss.

"It doesn't matter. You have come to New York from Reading, so you are the guest of America, and you deserve a gift," Michelangelo said as mom nodded to him approvingly.

"Well then, thank you for the gift." Elizabeth happily took the mouse doll, hugged it vigorously, then put it into her mother's arms and said to Michelangelo, "I have been learning aerobics. Let me show you an aerobic dance as a gift." After speaking, Elizabeth performed an energetic aerobic dance. She also improvised several unique movements for Michelangelo, which made him and the two mothers laugh.

After the dance, Elizabeth returned to her seat amid their applause, holding the mouse doll that her mother handed to her. Her face flushed. She and Michelangelo looked at each other and giggled.

When arriving at the station, Michelangelo pulled on his mother's arm. "Mom, can we get off a little later? I want to look at the mouse doll for a while longer."

After a while, Elizabeth and her mother arrived at their stop. Elizabeth pulled at her mother. "Mom, can we get off a little later? Michelangelo wants to look at this mouse doll for a while more."

Just like that, one station after another, they kept sitting in the car.

—

Time passed unconsciously.

One day a year later, a woman pushed into the car. She looked at Michelangelo and Elizabeth and said to the two mothers, "Your children are of school age, aren't they? I am from the Bright Futures School. You should enroll your children in our school for a better future! You all know California, right? It is such a wonderful developing country! Although we all love the United States, it is an underdeveloped country after all. You should enable your children to receive a better education in a developing country. Our school's goal is to help your children climb over the Great Wall and land in California!"

CHAPTER 2

THE GREAT WALL

Knowing that her mother could not afford the high tuition fees, Elizabeth told her that she didn't want to go to the Bright Futures School. Michelangelo reluctantly bid farewell to Elizabeth and her mother. He followed his mother, took a plane, transferred to a bus, and trudged a long distance to arrive at the Great Wall—the border wall between the United States and California in Nevada, a western state of the United States.

There were many small facilities on the Great Wall. They had different functions: some as classrooms; some as dormitories;

some as canteens; some to help climbing.

After his mother went through the admission procedure for him, Michelangelo started school life at the Great Wall. When a teacher taught in a one-person facility, each student studied in the one-person facility that surrounded the teacher. The student dormitory also only accommodated one person. Facilities with different functions, such as libraries and bars, could mostly accommodate only two people: an operator and a customer.

Michelangelo's mother commissioned the Thumb Organization to build a luxurious ballroom that accommodated a dancer and an audience. Her pole dancing business boomed. Sometimes, several audiences were waiting in line at the climbing facilities. She placed a long-term order to the Thumb Organization to move her ballroom up as her son moved to higher classrooms.

Every Monday to Friday, Michelangelo had to go to several facilities to take courses with different teachers. The school also added some climbing courses; these courses took the place of Physical Education in regular schools. Students did not need to take Physical Education because climbing on the Great Wall was a useful form of exercise.

The school also organized a choir. Because too few students signed up, Michelangelo was forced to participate after being selected by a lottery. He had no choice but to bite the bullet. He had to memorize the lyrics—if anyone opened his or her mouth without making a sound, points would be deducted from the final grade in the class. Members of the choir recently practiced a song named "Who Can Save the Poor California Kids" to support children living in hellish California. Michelangelo could not remember the lyrics because the title of this song confused him. *The admission advertisement stated that California's education and living standard were much better than those of the United States, but the textbook encouraged American children to prepare to join the great American effort to save California people who, it was claimed, were living in hell.* Michelangelo didn't know which one he should believe: *The admission advertisement or the textbook?* He did not understand why happy American children had to climb such a high Great Wall to arrive in hellish California.

—

Ten years later, 18-year-old Michelangelo climbed the Great Wall to reach 3,000 meters above the ground. According to the school's mission statement, the student who rose to this height would get a diploma.

At the graduation ceremony, looking back on the years of student life, the school, students, and parents were very emotional; many people shed tears of excitement. The graduation ceremony ended with singing "Who Can Save the Poor California Kids."

After the ceremony, the graduating students brought out their parachutes in preparation of landing in California.

"But," said someone, "where is the top of the Great Wall?"

It was Iron Mask, one of Michelangelo's classmates; he was a few years older than Michelangelo. To Michelangelo, Iron Mask was a weird person. From the day of enrollment, he carried ten hammers and ten chisels on his back every day. Moreover, holding a "TV set" with a monochrome screen all the time. This "TV set" was very similar to the one in the subway car back then; Iron Mask regarded it as a treasure. Michelangelo rarely communicated with Iron Mask because he was worried that it would hurt Iron Mask's heart if he accidentally told him the truth about the fake TV set.

Following Iron Mask's question, other people were also clamoring and wanted the school to explain.

"Maybe the wall has grown taller, just like the children," the school answered after a lengthy discussion.

Everyone looked up at the clouds that had flooded the upper part of the Great Wall. They began to complain to each other, "Why didn't you look up earlier?"

Someone suggested engaging a lawyer to sue the school, which got a unanimous response; however, everyone was silent again after learning about the retainer fee.

"Our children have studied hard for so long, but we can't even know where the endpoint is," someone murmured.

"If my child continues to climb, there are

no facilities there. Even if there are, who can take another ten years?" someone shouted.

"What if I send us to California with a manned spacecraft?" Iron Mask said.

"A manned spacecraft? Are you crazy? Do you know how much it costs to build a spacecraft and how long it takes?" someone shouted.

"What if I have one now?" Iron Mask said.

"Well, even if you have a spacecraft, let's talk about it first. How much will you charge?" someone said.

"The charge is fifty-six million dollars per person. If you already have a spacesuit yourself, you only need to pay fifty million dollars, so that way you can save six million dollars!" Iron Mask said.

"Who owns a spacesuit? However, even if we do own spacesuits, who can afford fifty million dollars? Of course, it's cheaper than the retainer fee, but we still can't afford it!" someone shouted.

"A special offer today: if you pay within fifteen minutes, you only need to pay two hundred dollars per person; if you pay after fifteen minutes, each person still has to pay fifty-six million dollars," Iron Mask said.

Everyone cheered and rushed to pay. In a short while, Iron Mask collected all the five thousand six hundred dollars.

Iron Mask pointed to the wall and said, "Now, as long as you remove a few stones here, you can board the spacecraft!" After speaking, Iron Mask selected ten strong men from among the students' parents and promised to pay each of them twelve dollars per hour. Iron Mask untied the ten hammers and ten chisels from his back and distributed them to these men. Iron Mask instructed the men to pry off a few stones and move them to a few abandoned facilities nearby. Almost five hours later, a hole large enough for a person to pass through penetrated the Great Wall; a hot wind blew through this hole from the other side of the Great Wall.

"But there is no spacecraft here?" someone asked.

"However, now you can reach the destination!" said Iron Mask. "Is it faster to go through this hole than to take a spacecraft? This hole is more valuable than a manned spacecraft."

"It turns out that you sold such a hole for five thousand six hundred dollars?" someone shouted.

"This hole is only worth six hundred dollars, and I've already let you earn it back. As for the five thousand dollars, it was used to pay for the idea of digging holes; I deserve it. Do you know about intellectual property rights? They are protected by law! If you didn't believe in it, you could have hired a lawyer to pay the retainer fee for a consultation," Iron Mask said.

"Well, even if you deserve five thousand dollars, now you can get through this hole without spending money; other students had to spend money—it is not fair!" someone shouted.

"No, I won't go through the hole because I have decided to give up landing in California," Iron Mask said. "I have decided to stay in the United States. Today I learned how much Americans like giving me money! Only a fool would go to a place where there are no Americans!" After that, Iron Mask waved to everyone and facing toward the United States, he jumped down. As his parachute opened, everyone heard his cheerful singing voice grow farther and farther away; the song he sang was "Who Can Save the Poor California Kids."

Iron Mask's happiness made everyone unhappy. Although the door to the new world had been opened to the graduates, they felt lost at this historic moment which should have been celebrated.

The students said goodbye to their parents in tears. Michelangelo hugged his mother. Then, carrying the parachute, Michelangelo followed his classmates through the hole and jumped down towards California. The parachutes opened and landed on California land one by one.

On California land, Michelangelo and his classmates looked up at the Great Wall's new side, looking for the California students studying on the wall. However, there was nothing there; there were only two lines of big blood-red words on the wall:

WELCOME TO DEATH VALLEY!

ONLY THE DEAD CAN GET OUT OF HERE!

Michelangelo and his classmates looked

ahead; it was a hot and desolate land. They suspected that they had not reached the dreamland but rather had opened the door of hell.

CHAPTER 3

DEATH VALLEY

Death Valley had the hottest ground during the day and the darkest sky at night. Michelangelo and his classmates finally believed that the textbook was correct: CALIFORNIA IS HELL. However, everyone had to choose to go to hell because they had no way to get back to the Great Wall's other side.

After walking in "hell" for seven days, Michelangelo was the only living person—the other students had fallen to the ground and turned into corpses. Michelangelo was still alive because he had covered his body with the heavy parachute—this reduced the damage caused by the harsh hot desert climate; however, the parachute could not serve as food and drink.

On the morning of the eighth day, Michelangelo woke up in the parachute. He had had nothing to eat for three days and nights and no water to drink for one day and night. As he moved on, he found something terrible: several corpses of his classmates appeared in front of him again—he remembered that he had passed them before. When he passed the corpses again trembling, he noticed some long drag marks on the ground, which meant they had been dragged by something. *Who dragged these corpses?*

However, Michelangelo was not interested in searching for the answer because he was dying.

Meanwhile, Michelangelo's mother had returned to New York. The news of a meteorite falling in New York was being reported on TV. It made her feel at ease that her son had left this dangerous country; she did not know that her son was wrapped in a tattered parachute alone on California soil, listening to the footsteps of death coming toward him.

—

Night fell, Michelangelo thought he was dead because the hunger and thirst suddenly disappeared, as did his body weight. He felt himself passing through the parachute and floating up slowly. Although there was no light around, he could see everything. He floated upward along the Great Wall, faster and faster, passing through the sky. He viewed the top of the Great Wall above the sky, which was a place over-looking the earth. He found some phantoms sitting on the top of the wall; they were facing the United States, immersed in colossal darkness.

Michelangelo recognized that those phantoms were his classmates who had died in Death Valley. Like him, their souls escaped from their bodies and could fly freely. Perhaps they were looking at their homeland; perhaps they were reminiscing about their days as living people; perhaps they were gazing at someone they love deeply.

Michelangelo learned from several phantoms' conversations that some souls landed on the ground at night, trying to drag their bodies to a place with water. Because it was too late to return before dawn, they all evaporated in the sunlight. So Michelangelo understood why those bodies had moved.

A soul hummed "Who Can Save the Poor California Kids" and several phantoms joined in; Michelangelo unconsciously sang along. Gradually, all the phantoms sang together. At this moment, this song expressed their nostalgia, and its original intention had no meaning. Sad singing enveloped the phantoms sitting on the high wall and everything plunged into deep darkness.

In the singing, school life seemed to reappear in front of Michelangelo. When the memory was frozen at his mother's loving and caring smile, in an instant Michelangelo felt as if he had already come to a nightclub. The lights there flashed wildly; his mother was dancing a very physically demanding pole dance; the audience there was joyful and crazy.

Seeing the hardship his mother endured, Michelangelo decided to live because he didn't want his mother to hear the news of his death one day. While thinking of this, Michelangelo felt that he had crossed the Great Wall and returned to the parachute covering his body.

Michelangelo's soul hid in the parachute, dragging his body lying on another part of the parachute.

The sky was getting brighter. Protected by the parachute, Michelangelo's soul still had a hard time dragging his body in the sun as the parachute did not completely block the sun. Although Michelangelo's soul was trying to persevere, he was getting weaker and weaker.

In front of him, there was a giant snake that opened its mouth. Michelangelo's soul desperately needed a shady place, so he dragged his body into the snake's mouth.

—

Michelangelo's soul dragged his body and walked inside the snake's slippery body. He vaguely saw the light appearing in front of him. The further he went, the brighter the light; however, this light did not hurt him. The flowers in this place were endless and the wonderful music came from nowhere. The people here were naked, covering their private parts with a few leaves, vying for apples from the air.

Michelangelo's soul found a man in clothes sitting in the flowers, one who did not fight for apples like the others.

"Hello," said Michelangelo's soul.

"Welcome to the Hotel California," the man said.

"I remember I entered the body of a giant snake. Why is this place called the Hotel California?" Michelangelo's soul asked.

"Because it's like California, people who come here like to stay here and do not want to leave anymore," the man said.

"Why are those people scrambling for apples?" asked Michelangelo's soul.

"Because they are inside the snake, the snake is making them do it," the man replied.

"But, aren't you also in the snake's body?" Michelangelo's soul asked.

"Because I know this giant snake was accidentally imagined by an arrogant guy, I am not confused by it. I am trying to imagine a giant eagle bigger than this snake; if this giant eagle appears, it will swallow the snake," the man answered.

"But if the giant eagle swallows the giant snake, won't you, me, and these people also be swallowed?" Michelangelo's soul questioned.

"No. The snake came from imagination; if the eagle appears, it will also come from imagination. Neither of them exists. Therefore, if the eagle swallows the snake, no one will get hurt," said the man.

At this moment, the world seemed to be distorted, and everything was shaking. Michelangelo's soul was being rolled around as if it were in a rolling cylinder.

"That's fucking awesome!" the man shouted. "I had been trying to concentrate on meditation, but I never succeeded. Just now, because I was distracted by talking to you, it worked! It turns out that I was unable to succeed before because I was too deliberate with my meditation! Now the giant eagle is tearing the giant snake apart and swallowing it; we will be free soon!"

"That's troublesome!" Michelangelo's soul shouted. "If the snake is swallowed, I will be burned by the sun!"

"I can't control the eagle! You know, people can't control their imagination," the man shouted.

"I was going to drag my body to somewhere with water. Now it seems that both my soul and body will be destroyed," Michelangelo shouted.

"Why do you want to return to that weak body? You no longer feel thirsty and hungry; isn't it perfect?" the man asked.

"I don't want my body to die because I don't want my mother to hear about my death one day. I don't want to make her sad!" Michelangelo's soul shouted.

"Okay, that makes sense. I'll try to drag your body to a place with water," the man shouted.

"But how can I follow you? The sun will burn me. If I am destroyed, my body will not survive," Michelangelo's soul shouted.

"You can hide in my asshole; it's very shady, and the sun will not hurt you," the man shouted.

"Are you serious? Are you humiliating me?" Michelangelo's soul asked.

"It's not a joke. If the sun is your enemy, darkness and filth are your friends," the man shouted.

Michelangelo's soul then got into the man's asshole.

At this point, the shaking stopped, and there was sunshine all over the world.

—

The man walked for a long time and finally found water. He untied the parachute holding Michelangelo's body and poured water into its mouth. However, the body did not wake up.

The man said to Michelangelo's soul in his asshole, "Your body is too weak; water can't save it. I have to take it to a hospital." Before his voice had died away, the giant eagle flew over, grabbed Michelangelo's body, and flew away.

"Sure enough. Your imagination is out of your control," the man said to Michelangelo's soul in his asshole. "It seems that this giant eagle is taking your body to a hospital. However, before the sun goes down, you still have to stay in my asshole. Wait till night, and you can go out and look for your body."

CHAPTER 4

THE PHANTOM

The AI Health System was monitoring every Californian's physical condition in real time. Whenever someone needed help, the unmanned aerial ambulance would fly to find the patient and use the octopus-like soft manipulators to move the patient into a treatment cabin. Next, the unmanned aerial ambulance would send the patient to a suitable medical institution. People with no signs of life would be transferred to a floating coffin. Equipment one in the coffin would update the death information to the AI Californian System; equipment two would destroy the deceased's clothes; equipment three would collect the belongings of the deceased into a box; equipment four would spray a particular gas to clean the dead body; equipment five would produce an anti-corrosion material burial suit based on the deceased's body size—the suit was made in multiple parts and placed on the deceased from different directions. Although it had no seams, it seemed to have layers. Simultaneously, the system would contact the deceased's social connections.

After the funeral, the corpse would be transferred to the AI Celestial Burial Base. The equipment there would carbonize the corpse, compress it into a luminous object, and then launch it into space. Because every luminous object was launched to the same location in space, these countless luminous objects gathered into a single star. Californians called it "End Star."

When the unmanned aerial ambulance appeared above the giant eagle, it handed Michelangelo's body to the ambulance and disappeared.

According to the diagnosis of the equipment in the ambulance, Michelangelo's body was sent to Cedairs-Sinair Medical Center.

—

Cedairs-Sinair Medical Center floated in the Mid-Skity West area of Los Angeles, California's largest skity.

Michelangelo's body was transferred from the unmanned aerial ambulance to the treatment cabin that only accommodated one person. The equipment in the cabin destroyed Michelangelo's clothes.

According to a further diagnosis, the treatment cabin carrying Michelangelo's body was moved to the intensive care area. There, the cabin was docked next to the medicine pipes. The gas medicine was piped into the cabin and entered Michelangelo's body in his breath; the liquid medicine was compressed into a sharp stream and injected into Michelangelo's body. If the patient underwent surgery, the operation system's scalpels were also made of gas or liquid; fortunately, Michelangelo's body did not need an operation yet.

—

The night was coming. Because Michelangelo's body was so weak, the treatment was still going on. Michelangelo's soul hovered on the edge of the floating Cedairs-Sinair Medical Center. Below this building, there were forests and streams; some animals were simply living there, and some were creeping about. Although all these creatures were in the darkness, they did not hinder the vision of a soul.

In the meantime, another phantom was also there enjoying the night view of the earth; he was simulating the action of shooting a firearm at a barn owl in a tree.

The phantom noticed that Michelangelo's soul was looking at him. He stopped in a bit of embarrassment. "I used to be an actor; most of the characters I played were good at shooting."

"Is your body being treated there too?" Michelangelo's soul asked.

"Yes, my body is undergoing treatment. I am taking the opportunity to play for a while. Although I am 71 years old, I will not die—the treatment here is very effective," the phantom said.

"I heard that most souls are reluctant to return to their bodies after they are free. Is there anyone or anything you can't let go of?" Michelangelo's soul asked.

"What I can't let go of is the A-Star Award for Best Actor. I was an actor; I spent all my life acting in movies. I was nominated repeatedly; I attended the award ceremony repeatedly, but I never got this award! I cannot be consoled!" the phantom said.

"It's just an award; that's nothing," Michelangelo's soul said. "Unlike me, I worry that my mother will be sad for me. If not for this, I would rather be a ghost traveling freely, which is a pleasure that people with bodies cannot experience. You can travel! It will make you forget the award! Have you never been to New York? In that place, 'Giant Mice Pulling Subway Train' is a famous scene!"

"What the hell is the 'subway train'?" the phantom asked.

"In the United States, all buildings are built on the ground. Many cities have subways under the ground. The sun never shines there, so there are good places for a soul to travel," Michelangelo's soul said. "But only

New York subway trains are pulled by mice."

"That sounds like such a good place! Well, I have decided to go there and have a look! As for the award, the award"—the phantom approached Michelangelo's soul—"I'll leave this to you. I want you to win that award for me!"

"What? What are you talking about!" Michelangelo's soul was startled.

"What I'm saying is YOU—MUST—WIN—THAT—DAMN—A-STAR—AWARD—FOR—BEST—ACTOR—FOR—ME! I won't let you off until you WIN—THAT—AWARD!" the phantom pointed a finger like a gun at Michelangelo's soul and disappeared.

CHAPTER 5

WELCOME TO CALIFORNIA

Michelangelo woke up in the treatment cabin. The light's brightness and color were adjusted according to his pupils. After he adjusted to the world he had returned to, the cabin slowly stood up, turning him from lying to standing. Next, there was an unmanned aerial vehicle docked with the cabin. Then, a drawer popped out inside the cabin. It contained a suit customized by the system according to his physical and psychological information. Following the voice prompt, Michelangelo put on the suit. A 3D hologram of himself wearing this suit rotated in front of him. He looked at it and thought it was the best suit for him. A side of the standing cabin opened like a door. Following the voice prompt, he walked out of the cabin. Because the treatment included nutritional supplements, he was full of energy, neither thirsty nor hungry, and felt healthier than ever.

An aircraft flew up; it was spherical, surrounded by rapidly rotating fine particles. In Michelangelo's view, it looked very similar to Saturn in the American textbook. When it stopped in front of Michelangelo, the fine particles disappeared. After the aircraft door opened, Michelangelo followed the voice prompt to enter. According to the voice prompt, Michelangelo learned that the aircraft was called the "fried egg car."

When the fried egg car restarted, it was surrounded by fine particles that were spinning instantly. Michelangelo understood why he didn't look for the seat belt during the flight—because he did not feel any vibration. Obviously, in a fried egg car, the seat belt was superfluous.

—

For a short while, the fried egg car flew under a floating roof. It landed in the lobby of a building. Michelangelo got out of the fried egg car and looked around. On the wall of the lobby were a few large words: AI Californian System Service Center. A few fried egg cars were landing, a few fried egg cars were leaving, and a few people were sitting on the floating sofas moving in the hall.

Meanwhile, a sofa floated in front of Michelangelo. After he followed the voice prompt to sit on it, it began to move, left and right, up and down, and entered a room. The wall color in this room happened to be his favorite, Coca-Cola Red.

Just then, a 3D holographic figure of a person wearing a mouse costume and headgear appeared in the room. It was very similar to the mouse doll that the President had gifted him.

"Hello, Michelangelo! Welcome to California!" The voice of the "mouse" was the same as that of Elizabeth that year. Michelangelo understood these voices were generated by the system based on the recorded information retrieved from him in the medical center.

The "mouse" began to make an introduction:

California is a developing country with a land area of 155,959 square miles and a water area of 7,737 square miles. After adding you, the current population is 30,875,921. The principle national conditions are as follows:

1. The constitution of California is "Programming Rules." California's national management affairs are governed by the AI National Management System; there are no human leaders at any level. The system analyzes each Californian's physical and psychological information in real time to make decisions about public affairs. No one is allowed to obtain anyone's data in this system. The system is subdivided into 1,144 subsystems involving safety, food, medical care, transportation, housing, etc.

2. There is no nationality system in California; all human beings in California have equal human rights.

3. In California, all animals are equal.

Humans are not permitted to domesticate animals or use animals for experiments. It is prohibited to define any animal as a "rare animal," "pest," "pet," or "beneficial insect."

4. In California, people can eat and use any animal products. The premise is that people are not permitted to use weapons and technologies that most animals cannot use. People can voluntarily land on the ground, but they must be naked like other animals. They can only cover their private parts with leaves. She, or he, can only defend or attack with natural objects, such as stones and branches. No organizations and individuals in the air are permitted to assist and rescue people on the ground. The work area of the unmanned aerial ambulance does not include the ground.

5. California land does not belong to any individual or organization. No buildings are permitted to be built on the ground; any building must be suspended in the air. Buildings are planned and constructed by the AI Building System. Their air positions are scheduled in real time based on population flow.

6. In California, all vehicles must travel

in the air. They are only permitted to land vertically and are not permitted to drive on the ground.

7. Children in California must and can only receive three years of universal education, including seven standard courses such as life knowledge, language, logic, and AI knowledge. The school-age for girls is six, and that for boys is eight. After the courses are completed, the AI Learning System will assign each student a career direction according to their genetic characteristics and the learning situation and arrange for her, or him, to enter industrial schools for professional learning based on practical works. When girls reach the age of sixteen or boys reach eighteen, the AI Work System will arrange for her, or him, to join the industry guilds. Suppose an industry is eliminated or a new industry emerges. In that case, the AI Work System will change jobs for all related personnel based on genetic characteristics and work records.

8. California prohibits any exams but permits various honors to encourage industry practitioners to compete and make progress.

9. California's currency is the Avocado-

llar. The AI Reserve System is permitted to store avocados in a frozen state; commercial organizations are permitted to store avocados in a fresh way; individuals can only store avocados at room temperature. California does not establish private deposit institutions. If some avocados rot, they will no longer have a currency function and be recycled by the AI Reserve System.

10. In California, no product is permitted to be advertised, and packaging boxes is not permitted. All products are delivered directly to the user by an unmanned aerial vehicle matching its size. Anyone who buys any product can only make a reservation with the production system one hour in advance. Anyone who reserves consumables shall not exceed the amount used within 24 hours.

After listening to this, Michelangelo was depressed. *Mom worked so hard to help me come to California, expecting me to get a better education; however, there is no university at all here!*

The system analyzed him and determined that Michelangelo had language, logic, and other necessary abilities. Based on his genetic characteristics, the AI Working System decided to assign him to the Sculptors Guild.

At this moment, Michelangelo suddenly lost consciousness.

—

As Michelangelo woke up, the "mouse" reannounced that he was assigned to the Actors Guild based on the system's latest evaluation.

Michelangelo was puzzled. At this point, he found a phantom in the corner of the room.

"Is that you? What did you do to me?" Michelangelo shouted.

"Shhh! I just possessed you for a while and showed off your performance talent on your behalf. It worked well! The system may think that your efforts have made up for your genes' limitations, so it has changed your career. You are still young, and you have plenty of time to win that award for me. As I said, if you can't realize my dream, I won't let you go! By the way, I went to visit your mother for you; she danced well!" The phantom disappeared after speaking.

CHAPTER 6

MOUSE PAIRK

California's industry system that combined learning and practice allowed Michelangelo to act in the role of different characters when he started to learn acting.

The word "movie" originates from the audience's actions. The audience of this kind of art is generally "on the move" to watch it. "Movie" is a 3D holographic audio-visual art form shown in any brightness and watched from any position. This art's predecessor is the ancient multi-perspective stage play. The center stages of the theaters of the ancient multi-perspective stage plays were generally four-sided, six-sided, eight-sided, or circular. The auditoriums of this kind of theater were circular, and the audiences could choose different regional seats. The seats in each area could only offer a view of one side of the stage. Therefore, some enthusiastic audiences watched the same show repeatedly in different seating areas until they got the whole plot.

Nowadays, the seats for watching movies can float and move, which allows the audiences to watch in fixed positions or on the move. For mobile audiences, the trajectory they move in for each movie is unique, so the plot they watch is also unique. Compared with the ancient, multi-perspective stage play, the movie plots are more complicated, and the audiences' experiences are richer. Whether it is a movie or an ancient play, the multi-perspective art form intuitively expresses the world's complexity.

—

In 1993, Michelangelo was nominated for A-Star Award for Best Supporting Actor for the movie *What's Eating Avocados.* It made him eligible for a role in the "protagonist group." In a movie, the audience at different positions follows different storylines; the different storylines' role assignments are different. Maybe watching from a certain position, a certain role portrays a protagonist, but watching from another place it becomes a supporting role. Even watching from a certain position, the audience thinks a certain character is a hero, but watching from another place, the character appears to be an antagonist. The so-called "protagonist group" refers to characters who are the protagonists in at least one storyline. The A-Star Award is the most authoritative in the movie industry in California; receiving this award is the most desired honor for every movie professional. Only those who have played roles in the "protagonist group" are eligible for the A-Star Award for Best Actor.

—

In 1996, the movie *The Tragedy of a Californian Falling in Love with an American,* starring Michelangelo and actor Airie Cairrie, was a huge success. Although Michelangelo was not nominated for the A-Star Award for Best Actor, he was remunerated in more Avocadollars. He worried that these avocados would rot and lose their value, so he decided to eat them all. To eat so many avocados, he had to do a four-count burpee his mother taught him every five minutes while eating to promote digestion. Airie Cairrie disliked Michelangelo's behavior very much. She could not tolerate someone eating money, and she thought it was quite abnormal. Therefore, when the famous director Games Gamer invited Michelangelo and her to co-star in the movie, *The Crash of a Manned Spacecraft,* she resolutely refused. Instead, she starred in *If California Has Lawyers,* a niche movie, with the unknown actor Madd Damon.

Michelangelo felt a little bit lost about it. He needed to relax, so he took a fried egg car to the Mouse Pairk. Interestingly, there were no mice in California, but there was a mouse-themed pairk. The "mice" in Mouse Pairk were people wearing mouse costumes and headgear. Although these actors who acted as mice did not need to show their faces, they had to be members of the Actors Guild to be qualified for this job.

Mouse Pairk was a favorite place for children. There were many amusement facilities; some rides were too exciting and caused them to scream. Movies were shown in the air, mostly fairy tales depicting the world of mice. There were no seats in the movie area; the children happily drove fried egg cars with two big simulated mouse ears, moving to watch movies.

Michelangelo met a cute "mouse," precisely the same as the "mouse" he met at the AI Californian System Service Center. Michelangelo was a little confused. *Can the system analyze my future events by scanning my brain? Are things about to happen in my mind in advance?*

When the "mouse" found Michelangelo, it seemed to be taken aback. However, it quickly returned to normal and began to dance aerobics. Michelangelo was stunned. *It is the aerobic dance Elizabeth performed in the subway car!*

After dancing, the "mouse" did the unique movements that Elizabeth had invented for

Michelangelo.

"Oh my God! Are you Elizabeth? How did you come to California?" Michelangelo shouted, going to take off the "mouse's" headgear. The "mouse" kept dancing while avoiding Michelangelo's hands.

Michelangelo shouted to the "mouse," "I will star in a movie called, 'The Crash of a Manned Spacecraft.' The heroine is still missing. You go to Hollywood to find the director named Games Gamer. He has always been obsessed with aerobic dance, so you will be selected!"

CHAPTER 7

VANISH INTO THIN AIR

In 1997, the movie *The Crash of a Manned Spacecraft,* starring Michelangelo and Elizabeth, made a California sensation, and they became California's most popular stars. "I'M THE KING OF THE UNIVERSE," Michelangelo's line in this movie, became a popular catchphrase.

In early 1998, the movie professionals were gathering in the Skyline Auditorium of Michael Angelo Jackson Skreet in Hollywood, a neighborhood in the central region of Los Angeles. The new A-Star Awards ceremony was being held to recognize the previous year's outstanding movies.

Following tradition, the tactile virtual avatars of the late A-Star Award for Best Actor winners sat in the first three rows of the guest seats. To protect the career opportunities of living actors, the Actors Guild prohibited virtual avatars of the dead actors from starring in movies but permitted them to attend the awards ceremony as guests. These avatars looked precisely like living people; if you shook hands with them, you could feel that their body temperature was the same as living people. The only difference between them and living people was that each of them had a bright halo behind her or his head. It was said that these bright halos were antennas that received control signals. These halos made these avatars look sacred.

The Crash of a Manned Spacecraft lived up to expectations and won several A-Star Awards, including an A-Star Award for Best Actor. The winner of Best Actor was not Michelangelo; however, he was still delighted because it was Elizabeth.

Elizabeth stood up excitedly and embraced the people around her, especially Michelangelo. She walked onto the podium amid feverish applause; the dazzling lights illuminated her highlighted moments. Michelangelo noticed that a man in the audience was distraught; it was Madd Damon. Madd Damon starred in *If California Has Lawyers* with Airie Cairrie; he was also nominated for the A-Star Award for Best Actor this time. Michelangelo immediately hated Madd Damon because he realized that although Madd Damon kept a polite smile, his eyes revealed deep jealousy for Elizabeth.

Elizabeth took the trophy excitedly from the avatars of the two late winners Grogory Pock and Aodroy Hopborn. She hugged the two avatars and gave an acceptance speech. "I feel very fortunate to have made it all the way from there to here," she said. "And I'd like to thank some of the people along the way who had faith...faith..." Suddenly, Elizabeth shook a few times and then disappeared. The trophy fell on the podium. The men at the scene were dumbfounded, and the women screamed.

Yes, Elizabeth, the winner of the A-Star Award for Best Actor, vanished into thin air.

—

As night fell, Michelangelo was riding in a fried egg car, holding Elizabeth's trophy in his arms. He flew everywhere Elizabeth might go to find her.

"It's not necessarily a bad thing," said the phantom who was sitting on the rapidly rotating fine particles around the car. "It may indicate that she has recovered."

"Why are you here? What are you talking about?" Michelangelo was a little angry.

"To come to California to find you, she worked on the Great Wall to make money while teaching herself to climb. She slept on some abandoned facilities every night. One day, she fell off the Great Wall due to a weakness in the structure. The serious injury turned her into a vegetable. What you met in California was her soul," the phantom said.

"But I met her in the sun!" Michelangelo shouted.

"She was hiding in the mouse costume and headgear," the phantom said.

"But while the movie was being shot, we were often exposed to the sun!" Michelangelo shouted.

"There are many ways for a soul to keep its living image from being burned by the sun, but no one would use these methods because they are excruciating. For a soul, it is like being in purgatory," the phantom said. "God knows how she fooled the system to join the Actors Guild—it is much harder for a soul to fool AI than to fool people. To achieve this, she had to suffer double pain."

"I want to go back to America to find her!" Michelangelo shouted.

"No, you haven't finished the task I gave you. Moreover, California and the United States are separated by the Great Wall!" said the phantom.

"Then, I want to commit suicide! You can't force me to win the award if I die! After death, my soul can cross the Great Wall and return to the United States!" Michelangelo shouted.

"You'd better have a bit of common sense. Only those who don't want to die will have free souls after their bodies die; for people who want to die, their souls will die along with their bodies. After all, everything is born of intention," said the phantom.

Michelangelo stopped talking and started sobbing.

"If you commit suicide, as you said, your loved ones will hear of your death one day, and they will fall into endless grief and despair. Do you want that to happen?" said the phantom. "However, if you want to stop me from pushing you, there is a simple way: You give me this trophy, and our agreement can be terminated."

"Don't even think about it," Michelangelo said. "It belongs to Elizabeth. No one can take it! I will give you the trophy you want!"

CHAPTER 8

THE DYING ART

Because of Elizabeth's disappearance, Michelangelo was in despair all day long. He didn't want to believe what the phantom told him; he wished it was just a lie.

One night, Elizabeth appeared in his dream. She was climbing the Great Wall, where all the facilities were sturdy. It was because Iron Mask's real purpose for giving up entering California was to stay on the Great Wall as a volunteer, using his ten hammers and ten chisels to repair any broken facilities. Therefore, no matter which facility Elizabeth slept in, she would never fall off.

After waking up, Michelangelo wrote this dream into a movie story named "Iron Mask," telling the story of Iron Mask volunteering to repair the Great Wall's facilities. Michelangelo did not write Elizabeth into this story because he continued to wish that Elizabeth had never climbed the Great Wall so that she would never have fallen off the Great Wall.

Michelangelo sent this story to several movie studios. Their AI actuarial system calculated the same rating for this story: Extremely Boring/Not Recommended.

—

In the following years, Michelangelo continued to star in movies such as *The Avocadiator, Blood Diavocadollars, The Avocadiator of Avocadollar Skreet.* He was nominated for the A-Star Award for Best Actor many times and never won. However, every time he felt lost, it was because the heroine was not Elizabeth.

Sometimes, Michelangelo carried Elizabeth's A-Star trophy on his back to the Mouse Pairk. He imagined that the "mouse" would appear in front of him again and perform that graceful aerobic dance.

But it never happened again.

—

One day in 2015, after the sun set, 41-year-old Michelangelo came out of the Mouse Pairk with Elizabeth's A-Star trophy on his back and was about to call a fried egg car.

"You can't always be in this state of mind," a voice said.

"Why it's you again? Can't you let me be alone for a while?" Michelangelo did not look at him.

"You are wasting my time. I am a soul, and I shouldn't stay in your world for so long. Your procrastination year after year will cause me trouble!" the phantom said.

"I have tried my best, and it's not my final decision whether I win the award or not. What can I do?" Michelangelo shouted.

"Whether you win the award depends on your performance. As a professional, you certainly know the fairness of assessing this award! Each audience seat records the audience's physical and psychological reactions during the entire viewing process. The selection system's statistics are accurate in monitoring every pupil change, heartbeat, breath, smile, and sigh of each member of the audience. None of your outstanding performances will go unnoticed; similarly, none of your mediocre performances can be erased," the phantom said.

"Have you ever thought that an actor's performance often depends on the professional level of the director? How can I control that?" Michelangelo shouted.

The phantom was silent for a while and said, "I'll be the director for you. I have accumulated decades of experience in acting, so I know how to activate an actor's potential. The key is that I have a wealth of experience in participating in the award process. I know what to do to help an actor be more likely to win the award."

"As a soul, how would you become a director? Would you try the painful method?" Michelangelo asked.

"There is a painless way to make a soul

move safely in your world. That is to possess someone's body," said the phantom.

"What would happen to the possessed person?" Michelangelo asked.

"His soul would be in shock temporarily. However, when I leave his body, his soul will wake up. Didn't you experience it back then?" said the phantom.

Michelangelo glared at him. "Don't you think it is impolite?"

"Maybe a little bit. However, if I can win an A-Star Award for Best Director for him, would it be a good thing for him?" said the phantom.

"He may not be willing to win an award in this way, right?" Michelangelo said.

"No matter what, I will do it! The western movie style I am best at is a dying art in Hollywood now. I want to make this style come back and shock Hollywood! I want to make a purely Rated R western movie full of insubordination, blood, and desperation. I promise it will be seriously unsuitable for kids!" the phantom shouted.

CHAPTER 9

STATUE OF LIBERTY

A strange thing happened in Hollywood: A well-mannered art movie director rushed into a movie studio producer's office, waving his arms and telling of the idea of an earth-shattering R-rated movie. Within 15 minutes, the shocked producer decided to produce the movie.

The director appointed Michelangelo to star in this movie. After the movie shooting started, he tapped into Michelangelo's acting potential fanatically. He ordered Michelangelo to be naked, to wear only a leaf skirt to dodge the virtual beasts on the movie set. Although Michelangelo knew that the virtual characters were not real beasts, he still felt nervous and scared.

During the break, Michelangelo noticed that the leaf skirt was made of U.S. dollar bills! The director explained that these were movable leaves, which were natural resources hidden underground in California. They were not fixed on trees like ordinary leaves. For hundreds of millions of years, these leaves have been spewing out from tall natural pipelines and falling everywhere.

"Is this kind of high pipeline called a dollar tree?" Michelangelo asked.

"Almost. It's called a Coca Collar tree, because Californians call this leaf Coca Collar," the director replied.

"Did you ever see the U.S. dollar bills when you were in the United States?" Michelangelo asked.

"I did see them; someone put some in your mother's thong," the director replied.

Michelangelo was a little unhappy. He was silent for a while and said, "Don't you think it is strange? These natural products that have existed hundreds of millions of years ago turned out to be American currency with the portrait of the American president."

"I don't know why Americans use these leaves as currency," the director said. "But when I was in the United States, I saw a statue of a goddess holding a torch. It is very similar to the vein pattern on a certain part of these

Coca Collars."

Michelangelo looked at the Coca Collar skirt and said, "Why don't I remember the Statue of Liberty on the dollar bill?"

"Isn't that it?" The director pointed to a Coca Collar on the skirt.

"It's not the Statue of Liberty; it's just part of the clothes of President Washington," Michelangelo said.

"I don't know who President Washington is. I have only seen the Torch Goddess. However, it does not matter what it looks like. Everyone will recognize what they see based on their different fund of knowledge," the director said. "Since God created everything, it is normal for something created by God to appear on other things created by God."

Michelangelo became more confused about it: *Why are the things Americans are racking their brains to acquire just ordinary leaves in this country?* But this confusion would not last long because as the shooting of the movie continued, tension and fear would regain all his attention.

CHAPTER 10

THE ASTROLOGER

In 2016, the R-rated movie *The R*, starring Michelangelo, caused a sensation and was highly praised by the media: WESTERN MOVIE, HOLLYWOOD'S DYING ART, IS BACK!

In 2017, on the day before the A-Star Award ceremony, Michelangelo carried Elizabeth's A-Star trophy on his back and took a fried egg car to an astrology studio at 1735 N. Vine Skreet in Hollywood. The astrologer here was a blind woman in her twenties. People said that she had been blind since she was born, and she had understood astrology since she could speak.

"You are not here at the right time, Mr. DiCaprio, but come in please," a voice came from the room; the door opened itself.

Michelangelo was surprised that although he had not made an appointment, she knew he was coming.

The ceiling of the astrology studio was transparent. It was not an ordinary blind woman in front of Michelangelo—she had no eyes at all, and the part of her face that should have eyes was skin. Curiously, the woman was pressing something like a magnifying glass that Americans often use on her forehead, as if she were looking at the sky above the transparent ceiling.

"Hello, are you, hmm, viewing the stars?" asked Michelangelo.

"Yes," the astrologer replied.

"Can you view the stars even in broad daylight?" Michelangelo asked.

"Of course no one can see the stars in broad daylight. More than the failure to see stars, the truth is that their two so-called eyes are just the locks of their real eyes," the astrologer replied.

Michelangelo understood the astrologer's

words very well because he had had the experience of being out of his body. That kind of panoramic viewing was more comprehensive than what could be seen with ordinary eyes.

"So, are the stars you see the same as the stars that ordinary people see in the night sky?" Michelangelo asked.

"I don't think that people can see the stars, no matter whether in day or night. Because no matter whether there are stars in the universe, the human eye cannot recognize anything that far away. Most things that humans see are just illusions of their brain, especially the stars," the astrologer said.

"So, if I want to know if I can win the award tomorrow, what stars do I need to use for divination? Are they the ones in my hallucinations or the ones you see?" Michelangelo asked.

"Neither. Stars outside the sky cannot affect the destiny of people on earth, not even the ones in your mind," the astrologer said.

"So, I guess it is the End Star that affects our destiny?" Michelangelo asked.

"Of course not. No matter how bright it is, it is just a bunch of corpses; besides, the

End Star is also out of the sky," the astrologer said. "Only the stars that people can touch can affect their destiny."

"But who can touch the stars?" Michelangelo asked.

"You go out and walk to the right for two minutes. There are some terrazzo tiles with five-pointed stars on the sidewalk; every five-pointed star has the name of a celebrity. Do you know that place?" said the astrologer.

"Are you talking about the Hollywood Walk of Stars? Who doesn't know such a famous place? I have wished my name to placed there!" Michelangelo said.

"Only such stars that are stepped on by Californians all day can affect the destiny of Californians," the astrologer said. "That is the misunderstanding of humans: Even if the answer is under their feet, they will insist on looking up to the sky to find the answer."

"So what should I do now?" Michelangelo asked.

"After you arrive at the Hollywood Walk of Stars, walk around on those terrazzo tiles at will and think of the question you want to know the answer to. When there is a commotion between tourists and a busker dressed as a movie character, you stop. Then, you bow down to look at the name on the five-pointed star on the terrazzo tile closest to you, count how many letters her or his first and last name have, and then add these two numbers together. Then, you walk in the opposite direction of the conflict with the same number of steps as the sum. After the conflict is over, notice in which direction the tourists are leaving. Then, you add each digit of the year, month, and day of that day's date and take the sum. Take the same number of steps in the direction the tourists left. Then, you bow down to look at the name on the five-pointed star on the terrazzo tile closest to you. Finally, come back and tell me the first letter of the first name and the last letter of the last name," said the astrologer.

—

Michelangelo did as the astrologer said. The result was "A" and "E."

—

"The first letter symbolizes the predetermined destiny. The second letter symbolizes the change of destiny. 'A,' the first letter you got, is the first letter in alphabetical order; it means 'best.' So, in the preset destiny, you will win tomorrow. The second letter you got is 'E,' which means three planets are connected in a straight line. Because your first letter is 'A,' there must be the sun, the largest planet in our galaxy, among the three planets. The conclusion is: Tomorrow, you will win the award unless there is a three-planet conjunction," said the astrologer.

"You said that stars outside the sky would not affect the fates of people on earth. Does that mean that planets outside the sky can't change people's destiny?" As Michelangelo spoke, he found that the astrologer was motionless. Her "magnifying glass" was falling to the floor.

The transparent ceiling opened. An unmanned aerial ambulance drifted in and used the octopus-like soft manipulators to move her into the cabin. Then, the ambulance moved up slowly and flew away. The transparent ceiling closed.

CHAPTER 11

THREE-PLANET CONJUNCTION

The next day, the movie practitioners were gathering in the Skyline Auditorium. The new A-Star Awards ceremony was being held to recognize the previous year's outstanding movies.

Following tradition, the late Best Actor winners' tactile virtual avatars sat in the first three rows of the guest seats. The bright halos behind their heads made the scene sacred.

The Great Wall, written and starred by Madd Damon, won the Best Original Movieplay. Carrying Elizabeth's A-Star trophy on his back, Michelangelo sat in the guest seat and gracefully pretended to applaud. He hated this movie and Madd Damon.

As the phantom boasted, *The R* won the Best Director.

Two tactile virtual avatars of the late winners John Woyno and Agnos Moorohood presented the trophy to the director. After the director gave his acceptance speech excitedly, he shouted to the audience, "Next to you, Michelangelo, you must win Best Actor for me!"

Michelangelo immediately understood that the phantom was possessing the director again.

Then, it was time to announce the winner of the Best Actor. The presenters were 101-year-old Kark Daaglas and 80-year-old Jana Fanda, two living former winners. Kark Daaglas opened an ancient-style secret letter, took a look, and then handed it to Jana Fanda in a gentlemanly way. Jana Fanda smiled sweetly and read the letter, "The A-Star Award for Best Actor goes to Michelangelo DiCaprio, *The R!*"

Carrying Elizabeth's A-Star trophy on his back, Michelangelo walked onto the podium amid feverish applause. He held back tears of excitement and took the trophy, adjusted his breathing, and said, "For this day, I have waited so long..."

"WAIT! PLEASE WAIT A MINUTE!" a person yelled and rushed to the podium. Michelangelo recognized that it was Madd Damon!

But Michelangelo was surprised to find another Madd Damon still sitting in the guest seat. *Why are there two Madd Damons?*

"I am Watt Damon, the messenger of the A-Star Award evaluation system. According to the law, any statistics calculated during astronomical anomalies must be recalculated. Because a 'three-planet conjunction' has just occurred, the previous statistics have been recalculated. In this envelope is the latest legal and valid winning information!"

Watt Damon handed the new secret letter to Kark Daaglas. Kark Daaglas opened the letter, looked at it, and then handed it to Jana Fanda in a gentlemanly way. Jana Fanda smiled sweetly and read the letter, "The A-Star Award for Best Actor goes to Madd Damon, *The Great Wall!*"

Madd Damon walked onto the podium amid feverish applause. He held back tears of excitement and took the trophy, adjusted his breathing, and said, "For this day, I have waited so long! Thanks to my twin brother Watt Damon for sending this new letter at the critical moment. It is quite a dramatic scene! If this plot is the ending of a movie, I guess it would fall into the category of a stereotype because it is too satisfactory—this will prevent it from winning!"

The guests laughed knowingly.

Madd Damon went on to say, "Yes, *The Great Wall* does not have a happy ending. By the way, I want to declare that it is a fictitious movie. Any similarity of names, places, or events to the real world is purely coincidental. The 'Raphael DiCaprio' I played is a heinous character. His parents yearned for great California and led him to climb the Great Wall to escape the United States. The process was so difficult that he and his father had to eat his mother, who starved to death first. Later, to get out of Death Valley, DiCaprio killed his father. He peeled off his father's skin and put it on his body to reduce the damage caused by the harsh hot desert climate. He got out of Death Valley by drinking his father's blood and eating his meat and internal organs. Yes, it was a challenging character for me. I tried to break from my moral code, but it was still difficult to understand this character's viciousness. We produced this movie not to make audiences judge evil people like DiCaprio morally, but to tell everyone that they are also victims—the harsh environment in which they grew up breeds their evil." Madd Damon choked. The guests in the audience were also silent; some ladies shed tears.

Madd Damon adjusted his mood. "I have decided to use the Avocadollars I got from this movie to establish a charitable organization called 'May There Be No More DiCaprio in Human Skin in the World.' This foundation aims to appeal to Californians to help poor Americans. We will receive avocado donations every three days to ensure that the organization always has fresh Avocadollars. Now, I would like to invite every kind person to join me in singing *The Great Wall*'s theme song, 'Who Can Save the Poor Americans.'"

Following Madd Damon, the guests sang with great emotion. To maintain his demeanor, Michelangelo clapped his palms and opened his mouth, pretending to sing with the others. It reminded him of a bad moment in the school choir on the Great Wall.

CHAPTER 12

FRIAR HILL

Losing the award—to be precise, losing the award after winning it—was a big blow to Michelangelo. It was painful for a person to fail to get something, yet it hurt a hundred times worse to get something and then lose it.

In the following days, Michelangelo was thinking about a question seriously: *how to die without committing suicide?*

On this day, he came to the transparent swimming pool of the Wallwolf Airstory Hotel, floating in Beverly Hills, a skity surrounded by the skities of Los Angeles and West Hollywood. When he jumped into the water with Elizabeth's A-Star trophy on his back and viewed the beasts running on the ground through the swimming pool's transparent bottom, his thinking gradually became clear. Yes, the law did not prohibit human beings from setting foot on the ground, and no one did so because the ground was animal territory—however, he was not afraid of death at all now. If the beasts attacked him, he would fight to the end and show the greatest desire to survive. He had performed this kind of plot many times in the movies, and he thought his performance could even fool himself! He felt that this would make him believe that he did not want to die so that his soul would not die and could cross the Great Wall and reunite with Elizabeth and his mother. He did this for another reason. He thought that the beast would eat his body after killing him, so his body would never be resurrected. He was 43 years old, and he did not want to be tortured up to the age of 71 by the damn A-Star Award like that phantom.

—

Carrying Elizabeth's A-Star trophy on his back, Michelangelo took a fried egg car and flew across skities one after another. When he flew to Moro Beach in Newport Beach, a coastal skity in southern California, he believed it was his ideal destination.

After the fried egg car landed, the voice prompt said, "You can enjoy the beautiful scenery here, but it is not recommended that you get out of the cabin; there may be animals nearby that can hurt you. If you go out voluntarily, you must take off your clothes and use a custom Coca Collar skirt to cover your private parts."

Michelangelo insisted on his decision. After a while, an unmanned aerial vehicle flew to a dock with the car, and a Coca Collar skirt appeared in an open drawer in the cabin. Michelangelo took off his clothes, put on the Coca Collar skirt, carried Elizabeth's A-Star trophy on his back, and walked out of the car.

There were many landing or floating fried egg cars nearby; the people in these cars were here on vacation. Michelangelo was very excited when he thought that he was about to fight beasts. He had the idea to catch the first beast that pounced on him. No matter what it was, he would treat it as Madd Damon and beat it to death.

Many cars moved above Michelangelo as tourists in these cars rarely find anyone standing on the beach. Several coyotes stared at Michelangelo as they rarely found humans standing on the beach as well.

Michelangelo grabbed a handful of sand and threw it at the coyotes. "I KNOW WHAT THE FUCK YOU ARE! I KNOW WHAT THE FUCK YOUR NAMES ARE! EACH OF YOU IS CALLED MADD DAMON! EACH OF YOU IS THE FUCKING MADD DAMON! COME ON, COME ON, COME AND BITE ME!"

Those coyotes froze for a moment, then suddenly turned around and ran away.

Michelangelo looked up and saw that many cars were hovering above him—more tourists came to watch the fun.

"ARE THERE ANY ANIMALS THAT CAN FIGHT HERE? I WANT A COUGAR!" Michelangelo shouted to the cars gathered above him. "WHO CAN TELL ME WHERE THERE IS A COUGAR? I WANT THE MOST

FEROCIOUS ONE!"

Many tourists in the car pointed their fingers in the direction behind Michelangelo. A tourist opened the car window and shouted to him, "Hi! Be careful! Mr. Sirtallone, it's behind you!"

Michelangelo turned to find a muscular cougar staring at him. He suddenly felt that Madd Damon was not that important, and he was not in a hurry to fight any animals. He also thought that standing on the soft sand would make people's legs weak.

When the cougar pounced on Michelangelo, he wanted to show a little resistance, at least a scream; however, his body was no longer under his control.

—

The cougar pressed Michelangelo down onto the beach and opened its bloody mouth. Michelangelo found that although he wanted to die, he still could not face this process—death was indeed terrible for a living being.

Suddenly, Michelangelo felt his body relax, and the cougar let him go. The cougar stared quietly up at the sky.

Michelangelo could not figure out whether he was dead or alive. He felt the dazzling sun. He supported his upper body with his arm. He found a group of friars in dark brown robes walking silently in the air. When they reached the cliff of a hill next to the beach, the figures of these friar solidified into the cliff, much like a relief.

Just then, many animals came on the beach, ignoring Michelangelo, quietly staring at the figures on the "relief."

Michelangelo was feeling a sense of enlightenment. He had never believed in the existence of God like now. He thought that these friars gave him a new life; they must represent God's will. He was grateful to God for giving him a new life, just like what He gave to Adam. Michelangelo was so ashamed that he had wanted to give up the precious life given by God. He longed to make up for his blasphemy against God. At that very moment, he had an idea, which was to star in a movie about how God created Adam. He hoped that one day he could stand on the podium and tell the miracle in a glorious moment so that everyone could believe in the existence of God.

Many tourists got out of the car naked, wearing Coca Collar skirts, staring at the friars on the cliff with Michelangelo and the animals.

CHAPTER 13

IRON MASK

Carrying Elizabeth's A-Star trophy on his back, Michelangelo explained his new idea to several senior executives in a movie studio meeting room.

"I like this idea," one of them said. "So, what do you want?"

"I hope to play the most dazzling role in this movie," Michelangelo said.

The few people in the meeting discussed in a low voice and said to Michelangelo, "Deal."

—

Movie Pairk was the most prominent movie theme pairk in California. It floated in the San Flymando Valley area of Los Angeles. It provided tourists with many famous movie scenes, and it was also a place where movie studios held conferences. The press conference for the movie *From the Dust* was being held here. At the press conference, the movie studio's spokesperson announced the movie's cast. Madd Damon, the lastest winner of the A-Star Award for Best Actor, would play the part of Adam, and Michelangelo would play the part of God.

"What?" Carrying Elizabeth's A-Star trophy on his back, Michelangelo was stunned. He whispered to the senior executive next to him, "Didn't you promise me the most dazzling role?"

"We keep our promises. Is there any role more dazzling than God?" the producer said.

"But, according to the script, God only appears for a while, not even as a supporting role. Adam is the most dazzling protagonist!" Michelangelo said.

"But Adam was created by God. Do you mean God is less dazzling than Adam? Stop talking, or God will be angry!" the producer said.

After the announcement, all the reporters gathered around Madd Damon to interview him. Michelangelo walked away silently.

—

Carrying Elizabeth's A-Star trophy on his back, Michelangelo wandered along the Hollywood Walk of Stars. In the distance, a busker dressed as a movie character was arguing with several tourists. Not far away, a young bearded man stepped on a floating fried egg car to give a speech. He called for amendments to the Constitution so that the AI National Management System could successfully monitor the desire of the people and the animals of California to treat all lives equally.

When Michelangelo listened to the speech, he felt something moving on his feet. He looked down and found that it was a cute puppy scratching his shoe. Michelangelo was surprised. As far as he knew, California did not permit people to domesticate animals. There were only wolves in California, no dogs, and not even the word "dog" existed. Moreover, non-flying animals could not appear on the floating Hollywood Walk of Stars.

Michelangelo touched the puppy; it was cold. He realized that it was an AI toy dog. But Californians had never known about dogs. *Who made this toy dog?*

Michelangelo looked around. Except for a few tourists nearby looking at the puppy curiously, he did not find the toy dog's owner.

"Coin! Coin!" someone shouted.

It was Iron Mask's voice! Iron Mask was not born in American, so his accent was different from that of natural-born Americans.

The toy dog pressed on Michelangelo's shoe and barked at Iron Mask.

Iron Mask heard the barking and came over. "Hello gentleman, are you from America?"

"Hi, Iron Mask. I'm Michelangelo DiCaprio. Don't you remember me?" Michelangelo said.

"Oh, your appearance has changed a lot, and you no longer have a New York accent. If you didn't say your name, I would not recognize you. It seems that the toy dog I made is useful—I added a function to search for Americans," Iron Mask said.

"Aren't you working as a volunteer on the Great Wall to repair any broken facilities? Why did you come here?" Michelangelo asked.

"What are you talking about? How could I have spare time to repair any facilities? I built an 18-seat manned spacecraft that could fly over the Great Wall. Eight rich American couples booked tickets, but they worried about safety and insisted that I take a seat myself. So, I came to California," Iron Mask said.

"Then there should be one seat left. Did you waste a seat?" Michelangelo asked.

"No waste. The toy dog took that seat," Iron Mask said.

"But it didn't need a seat. It could just lie under the seat, right?" Michelangelo asked.

"Respect. Do you understand? It is called RESPECT. I made it, so it is part of my life. Any life must be respected," Iron Mask replied.

"It makes sense. By the way, are these eight rich couples still in California now?" Michelangelo said.

"Yes. But they are in a place where Californians don't dare to go!" Iron Mask said. "The day we arrived in California, they found that many tall pipelines were gushing out dollar bills endlessly. So they all went crazy and jumped down to the ground. I couldn't stop them. I don't know how they are now or whether they are still alive. In my view, upon seeing such a scene, even if there are deadly beasts, any American would jump down without hesitating."

"Then why didn't you do it? I remember you love dollars too," asked Michelangelo.

"I love money, but I understand that U.S. dollar bills are not money in California; they are just ordinary leaves," Iron Mask replied.

"So, have you considered shipping the dollar leaves here to the United States?" Michelangelo asked.

"Don't mention it. I spent many avocados on garbage disposal fees to clean up the huge pile of U.S. dollar bills that the eight rich couples paid to me. Besides, even if I can bring the U.S. dollar bills here to the United States, what useful things can I buy? Can I buy a house floating in the sky? Can I buy a self-driving flying car? Whenever I remembered that the United States was still in the era of humans driving cars, I was scared! Traffic conditions change rapidly. How do human brains respond? After repeatedly losing money, the guys on Wall Street realized that the impulsive human brain was unreliable and only computers that were always calm and unemotional could make transactions that were always profitable. However, they still chose to drove their cars by themselves after getting off work! What was the matter with them? Did they take it for granted that their lives were worth less than money?" Iron Mask said. "Compared with California, the United States is still a primitive society! Go back to the United States? Am I stupid? What I am thinking about now is how to send California's rich people to develop Mexico! I am developing a super manned spacecraft that can fly over the Mexican-California border wall!"

"What? Are you confused? California has no rich people," Michelangelo said.

"Oh, I overlooked that. Yes, individuals cannot keep avocados for a long time, so there are no rich people in California," Iron

Mask said. "Then I would position the service to give every Californian a chance to travel to Mexico!"

"But maybe Mexico does not permit Californians to enter at all!" Michelangelo said.

"It doesn't matter. I can change the slogan to 'Go to Mexico to Explore.' The word 'EXPLORE' accurately defines the uncertainty of this kind of travel, and this uncertainty can, even more, inspire people's desire for adventure!" Iron Mask said.

"But advertising is not permitted in California!" Michelangelo said.

"It's not an advertisement! It's a speech! It's a lead! It's an exciting verse!" Iron Mask said. "I suddenly had a bold question. You know, I came to California and found that there were U.S. dollar bills everywhere. So, if one day I arrive in Mexico, will I find that Mexico is full of avocados?"

"How is it possible? Many of my movie characters died for avocados. If there is a place with avocados everywhere, haven't these movie plots become a joke?" Michelangelo shouted.

"But Americans can never imagine a place

with U.S. dollar bills everywhere as well!" Iron Mask said.

"Okay, okay, I'm not in the mood right now! I don't want to argue with you about whether there are many avocados in Mexico!" Michelangelo said.

Iron Mask said thoughtfully, "However, since you just said that there were no rich people in California, I am interested in the challenge of being the first rich person in California. I can develop AI-controlled unmanned planting technology to grow avocado trees on the ground in California to form a large-scale Avocado Chain—"

Michelangelo interrupted him, "I beg you, don't continue to bother me! I am not interested in you being a rich man, and I am not interested in your Avocado Chain either!"

"Are you upset now?" Iron Mask asked.

"I am troubled. Can you leave me alone for a while?" Michelangelo said.

"That's great!" Iron Mask patted Michelangelo on the shoulder. "Now you can take a closer look at the face in front of you."

"What happened to your face? Did you have plastic surgery?" Michelangelo asked.

"No, no, no. I mean, the face in front of you is the smartest face in the world," Iron Mask said.

"I've heard that someone can have a smart brain, but this is the first time I have heard that someone's face is smart. Are you thinking with your face?" Michelangelo asked.

"I mean, the face is the appearance of the brain—the brain represented by my face is the smartest. After all, the brain is not exposed," Iron Mask said.

"According to you, it seems that hair would also represent the appearance of the brain. If it's bald, then the scalp is the appearance of the brain," Michelangelo said.

"Don't interpret my words in such a limited way; it's just a metaphor. I mean, you can tell me your troubles. If I can't give you a perfect solution within ten seconds, you can call me 'Idiot Mask'! Even 'the idiot from primitive society'!"

"Well, smart guy, listen up: I have a movie idea about God's creating Adam. The movie studio accepted my idea and agreed to let me play the part of the most dazzling role. Later, I learned that the role they gave me was 'God'.

In this movie, God is not even a supporting role! What should I use to compete for the A-Star Award for Best Actor? Come on! Tell me what to do in ten seconds! Ten, nine, eight, seven..." Michelangelo shouted.

"It's easy," Iron Mask smiled and pointed to the toy dog.

"What do you mean?" Michelangelo asked. "Are you going to let it bite them?"

"Of course not," Iron Mask said. "Let me ask you first, what is the name of it?"

"Its name? I heard you calling it 'Coin'," Michelangelo said.

"No, I mean, what kind of animal it is?" Iron Mask said.

"Dog!" Michelangelo said.

"Then what about 'dog' spelled in reverse?" Iron Mask asked.

"G—o—d, God? Oh, God! What are you trying to say?" Michelangelo said.

"You met this toy dog today; it was a revelation. It prompts you to reverse the story," Iron Mask said. "If God creates everything, then time is also created by Him, right?"

"It seems...that's it," Michelangelo rubbed his head.

"Since time is also created by God, God will not be limited by time. Therefore, from the birth of Adam, God created human beings, but if we go back from the Last Judgment to the Creation of Adam, isn't it a story of human beings leaving God step by step?" Iron Mask said.

"I think if I follow your thoughts, I will go crazy soon," Michelangelo said.

"That is the key. Audiences are looking for this kind of theme that would make them crazy. It doesn't matter whether this idea is reasonable or not. Audiences love it!" Iron Mask said.

"This idea is too much! Audiences like this kind of reverse brainwashing!" Michelangelo exclaimed. "I want to negotiate with the movie studio immediately. They will be shocked by this idea! They must ensure that I play the part of Adam and write it in the contract!"

"No, no, no!" Iron Mask said. "Don't go back to that movie studio. You have to go to its rival studio instead. Also, you must ask to play the part of God. Because in this story, God is the protagonist, and the other roles come and go quickly. Even Adam just has an unimportant role, and he only appears for a short while at the end of the movie."

"I have to say you are the sharpest thinking person I have ever met. I bet you can land in Mexico!" Michelangelo exclaimed. "I'm going to terminate the contract with that shit movie studio!"

"No, no, no!" Iron Mask said. "To thank you for your compliment, let me give you an added piece of advice: For that studio, you won't have to do anything."

"But in that story, God is just a cameo role!" Michelangelo said.

"Don't worry, that movie will never be produced," Iron Mask said. "After the movie plan of the next movie studio you are about to sign with is announced, the AI actuarial system of the previous movie studio you signed with will confirm that the new story of its rival will take away the audience of the original story. Therefore, they will cancel that project and, according to California law, pay you double avocados as compensation for all damages."

"Iron Mask, I want to take a serious look at you!" Michelangelo said.

"What?" Iron Mask asked.

"I want to take a closer look at THE SMARTEST FACE! I now firmly believe that Mexico is full of avocados!" Michelangelo exclaimed.

CHAPTER 14

MOVIE PARK

The spokesperson for the movie *Back to the Dust* announced that Michelangelo would perform the role of God in the movie. In all the storylines of the movie, each protagonist is played by the character, God. Michelangelo knew that this was his best chance to win the A-Star Award, and there would never be such a significant role offered to him again.

But who was able to act the part of God? No one had seen God, but God had an established image in everyone's mind. Michelangelo knew that there were at least a thousand and one images of God in the minds of one thousand people. Because in his mind, there were at least two images of God.

One night, carrying Elizabeth's A-Star trophy on his back, Michelangelo went for a drink at 8440 Sunset Blvd's transparent Skybar in West Hollywood. The beautiful scenery overlooking West Hollywood did not relieve him of the tremendous psychological pressure he was feeling.

When he called for a fried egg car to leave, a voice was heard and it said, "I will wait for you at Movie Pairk."

It's that phantom again! Michelangelo hesitated and ordered the car to fly to Movie Pairk.

—

Because it was night, Movie Pairk was closed.

"Come here," the phantom appeared. "I am a soul, so I can get in without a door, but you can't. There is a secret door here. It can be opened by saying the password."

"Why are you bringing me here?" Michelangelo asked.

"To improve your acting skills! No one has ever been challenged to act in the role of God. Just rely on your acting skills? Tsk tsk," said the phantom.

"Aren't you very proficient in acting? Even my career direction depended on your performance! Why didn't you teach me?" Michelangelo asked.

"I don't know how to act out the character God. Most of the characters I was good at were those who believed in rifles," the phantom replied.

"So, what is the password?" Michelangelo asked.

"MICHELANGELO DICAPRIO WILL NEVER WIN THE A-STAR AWARD FOR BEST ACTOR," the phantom replied.

"What are you talking about?" Michelangelo's eyes widened.

"I mean, the password is: MICHELANGELO DICAPRIO WILL NEVER WIN THE A-STAR AWARD FOR BEST ACTOR," the phantom said.

"Why did you set up such a password? Are you cursing me or humiliating me?" Michelangelo shouted.

"Shh—" the phantom said. "This password has been set for hundreds of years. It has nothing to do with you, and it has nothing to do with me. Since God created everything, all passwords and all names were created by God, so it's reasonable that any password could contain any name."

Michelangelo said the password awkwardly, and the door opened. He followed the phantom into the Movie Pairk.

—

"Are you familiar with this place?" the phantom asked.

"I've been here for several movie press conferences, but I haven't explored this area in any detail yet," Michelangelo replied.

"Many famous movie sets have been built here. Those sets made tourists feel like they were in a movie. However, this place was not built for tourists," the phantom said.

"Not for tourists? Why did they build a place like this?" Michelangelo asked.

"There is a rule in the Programming Rules: Before the system makes important decisions, it must finally be verified by people with a 'special ability to perceive humans,'" said the phantom.

"A special ability to perceive humans?" Michelangelo asked.

"A long time ago, after the AI analysis, an optimal solution was reached, which was that the people who had won the A-Star Award for Best Actor were recognized as the people who had a 'special ability to perceive humans.' Because their lifetime exploration was to observe people, experience people, and act as people. Their identities were kept secret; the system calls them 'secret people.'" The phantom pointed forward. "Look carefully, why are the movie sets built here all hills and slopes? Because only such terrain can accommodate a huge secret space hidden below. This place is dedicated to secret people; it is called Secret Skity. Whenever the system needs them, they will be gathered together here to observe the introduction of any draft proposals for pieces of legislation."

"So, are they the decision-makers?" Michelangelo asked.

"It's not like that. The system just scans

and analyzes their reactions to the case. The AI analyzed the entire human history and believed that any decision made by the human brain was dangerous. Due to the nature of human gene programming, human beings create many hallucinations in the brain that serve to protect their self-esteem, making them unable to perceive the world accurately and truly know them-selves. Even those secret people are no exception," the phantom said.

"Can't they participate in decision-making? Isn't it boring otherwise?" Michelangelo said.

"I think so. I didn't know this when I was alive. Now I know that I was lucky to miss this honor. Otherwise, how tortured this secret immortal life would be!" said the phantom.

"Immortal life?" Michelangelo asked.

"Yes, damn IMMORTAL LIFE!" said the phantom. "It means they can never fly freely."

"Then why can these people live forever?" Michelangelo asked.

"That is also a kind of death: social death. They can no longer communicate with the world as a living mortal. This is tough for a person," the phantom said. "It is also the reason many A-Star Award for Best Actor winners have enjoyed 'longevity'—they would give various reasons to delay the start of their 'social death.' However, the system did not permit them to live to an age that the public couldn't understand. Generally, if they delayed death until they were in their 90s, the system would arrange a fake death and then hold a funeral for a simulated wax corpse—now you know what the real business of the star wax museum in Hollywood is."

"So, like your situation now, is it also a 'social death'?" Michelangelo asked.

"No. I have been dead, but I just didn't go where I should go. It is also a kind of torment which can be referred to as being 'socially alive,'" said the phantom. "After I died, I was no longer obsessed with many things, including the award."

"Then, since you don't care about the award anymore, why are you still bothering me?" Michelangelo asked.

"I'm not reconciled to the fact that my whole life was tortured for such an award!" said the phantom. "I just want to enjoy that there is another fool like me in this world, which can give me a little comfort."

"A little comfort? All your fucking torment of me is just to get a little comfort? Why is your mind so dark?" Michelangelo roared.

"In everyone's mind, there is a dark side. I am a ghost now, so my dark area is wider than it is with living people," said the phantom. "By the way, ask yourself: Haven't you felt lucky that you had experienced a rich life playing different characters? Do you admit that the career direction I guided you to is wrong?"

Michelangelo was silent for a while and said, "So, those avatars who attended the award ceremony are..."

"They are certainly not avatars; they are those immortals. For them, participating in the award ceremony is a rare opportunity to return to society. Most of them like the moment, except for a few weirdos," the phantom said.

"But that is odd. They are not the right age; some of them looked much younger than they were when they died," said Michelangelo.

"Each human body's growth is set, and the current biotechnology can readjust this setting. However, the law does not permit this technology to be applied to ordinary people, except for the secret people. These secret people were set to their physical state as the age when they received their awards. The AI Secret People System considered it was the best solution," the phantom said.

"Since they are all living people, why install antennas for them?" Michelangelo asked.

"Those are not antennas; those are real halos. All people have halos behind their heads, but people's eyes cannot see the light of that wavelength. However, many biological characteristics of the secret people are already different from ordinary people. The light of the halos of secret people has become visible light," the phantom replied.

The phantom led Michelangelo through several movie sets. During the day, there were various virtual characters in these scenes. When the pairk closed at night, only these scenes were left. The phantom led Michelangelo through a set that looked terrifying, and it led into a secret entrance.

—

"Is it still far? Shall we call a fried egg car?" Michelangelo asked, after walking for a while on a dimly lit secret trail.

"The system believes that any accelerated object may increase anxiety for people who have plenty of time; so there are no vehicles in Secret Skity. Anyway, it is not a vast place; these secret people enjoy such leisurely stroll," said the phantom.

In front of him it was getting brighter. Michelangelo realized that he was in an unusual world.

"All the 'dead' A-Star Award for Best Actor winners in history are here. Whether you can get advice depends on your luck. I have to go; I don't want to meet these people." The phantom made a shooting motion at the Secret Skity, and then disappeared.

CHAPTER 15

SECRET SKITY

Carrying Elizabeth's A-Star trophy on his back, Michelangelo walked on the skreet in Secret Skity. The artificial sky here was divided into different colored geometric figures. According to the corresponding secret people's psychological and physiological data, the AI Secret People System changed every section of the sky in real time—one was sunny; one was filled with shining stars; one was full of flowers...

The system constructed different scenery and buildings based on each secret person's psychological and physiological data. The actors' memories made most of the buildings here resemble those in the movies they had starred in. The memories of different actors living on the same skreet made for the presence of different architectural styles.

As an actor, Michelangelo had studied many classic movies. Against the backdrop of the sky of various shapes and colors, Secret Skity's unique fantasy landscape made him feel pleasant and deeply fascinated.

—

A fashionable woman greeted him, "Hi, king of the universe!"

Michelangelo recognized that she was Soson Hoyword, an excellent actor of the middle of the last century! A beauty from another era greeting him with a line from his movie made Michelangelo very excited.

"Hello, Ms. Hoyword, pleased to meet you! I have come here to study! I loved your *I Want Avocados* very much! Could you tell me how I can deliver an outstanding performance in the role of God?" Michelangelo said.

Soson Hoyword smiled sweetly at Michelangelo. "Thank you for your compliment!

But talking about theatrical performance is a sacred thing. So I am sorry; it's not the right time."

Michelangelo remembered that according to historical records, Soson Hoyword liked astrology. She only did important things at 4:44 P.M. every day. Although it was a bit regretful that he missed the right time, Michelangelo felt in a good mood to have had the chance to meet this lovely woman.

—

After saying goodbye to Soson Hoyword, Michelangelo turned to another skreet and screamed in pain because his left hand was burned. He took a closer look, and it turned out that it was a lighted fashion cigarette floating nearby that had burned his hand. The cigarette was so long that he could not be sure where it originated.

Michelangelo followed along the length of the cigarette, went around several skreets, and finally found a teenage girl who was squatting on the skreet corner and smoking it. He tried to think of which teenage girl in history had won the A-Star Award for Best Actor.

"Hi, king of the nominees! What are you doing here? Are you here for the wedding of Aodroy and Grogory? It seems you are late." The "little girl" stood up; she was an adult woman. *How she could perform!*

Michelangelo recognized her as Gongor Rogors, one of his favorite actors, who became popular in the "Golden Age of Hollywood." Although being called "king of the nominees" made him a little embarrassed, thinking about the happy endings of the two legends also gratified him.

"Ah, nice to meet you, Ms. Rogors. Forgive me for not recognizing you just now. Your beautiful cigarette is so long!" Michelangelo said.

"If it is not long enough, how can I kill time?" Gongor Rogors replied.

"I envy you for having so much time. I'm going to be killed by time. I got a chance to play the part of God. The movie is about to start shooting, but I'm not ready yet. I'm going crazy! So I've come here to learn how best to perform the role of God," Michelangelo said.

"Acting as God? You need to observe God

first! But only after death can people meet God, right? Hey, I am afraid I will not have this chance," Gongor Rogors said. "However, if you want to learn how to act as a little girl, I can help a little bit."

Michelangelo thought it was indeed an experience he had never had, but that was not his top priority. So, he said goodbye to Gongor Rogors.

—

Michelangelo continued walking and found an ancient California style grand palace. The palace had no walls, no guards, no servants, only rows of tall pillars. On the majestic throne in the hall, a beautiful woman wearing a crown was sitting, looking at a piece of the heart-shaped sky burning with fire. *It is the young Elozoboth Toylor!*

Michelangelo felt nervous and was almost choking; he walked forward cautiously. Based on his experience in a classical movie, he saluted her in a manner reminiscent of the etiquette of days gone by. "It's nice to meet you! Ms. Toylor, I am Michelangelo DiCaprio.

Your character as the queen of ancient California is unforgettable! I wonder if you could teach me how to act out the part of the character of God."

"Are you going to play God?" Elozoboth Toylor glanced at Michelangelo, then continued to look at that piece of heart-shaped burning sky. "Why are you playing God? He created so many stupid men! Why are you asking a woman how to play God? You should ask those stupid men that God made! They believe they know everything! Teach you to play God? They would dare! They would absolutely dare to do this!"

—

After bidding farewell to the "queen of the movie," Michelangelo found a manned spacecraft-shaped bar with the same style as the one in *The Crash of a Manned Spacecraft* he had starred in. Michelangelo entered this bar and found a gentleman sitting there, drinking while reading an ancient paper book. Opposite him, there was a floating goblet. He touched it with his goblet and took a sip.

Captain! Michelangelo recognized it was the actor Goorgo Scott, who played the old captain in *The Crash of a Manned Spacecraft!* He looked much younger than before, about forty years old. Since the "death" of Mr. Scott eighteen years ago, Michelangelo had never met his "avatar" at the A-Star Award ceremony.

Michelangelo was a little nervous. He had experienced Mr. Scott's famous temper, but he was afraid of missing the opportunity to improve his acting skills. He stepped forward carefully. "Hello, Mr. Scott. How have you been? I am Michelangelo DiCaprio! Do you remember me?"

"You are here at the right time, boy, have a drink with me." Goorgo Scott motioned to Michelangelo to sit opposite him and motioned to him to pick up the floating goblet. Then he clinked his goblet with Michelangelo.

Michelangelo took a sip of wine and said, "This wine is awesome! Mr. Scott, I've got a chance to play the part of God. I want to use this character to win the A-Star Award for Best Actor, so I hoped you might teach me how to give an outstanding performance in playing God."

"What the hell! After so many years, is the world still like this? The selection of the A-Star Award is a goddamn meat parade. Only mules fight for it!" Goorgo Scott was angry.

Oops! I'm so stupid! Michelangelo suddenly recalled that Mr. Scott hated the A-Star Award since he was "alive." He had even refused to receive an A-Star Award. However, it did not prevent him from entering the list of immortals—it seemed that the system's authentication of the 'special ability to perceive humans' did not consider whether the winners themselves accepted the honor.

Goorgo Scott took a sip of wine and slammed the table. "Every dramatic performance is unique and cannot be compared to others."

Facing this angry senior, Michelangelo felt like he was sitting on pins and needles. He had to make an excuse to escape from there.

—

As soon as Michelangelo got out of the bar, he ran into a gentleman.

Michelangelo recognized this gentleman as the legendary actor Loonol Borrymoro, who had been active from the end of the nineteenth century to the mid-twentieth century. Loonol Borrymoro patted him on the shoulder and said, "Young man, I once watched the movie clip you starred in at the awards ceremony; I think you have chosen the wrong profession."

"Maybe you are right, Mr. Borrymoro. Unfortunately, I have fallen in love with this profession. I am desperate to know how to give an outstanding performance in acting the character of God. For God's sake, please enlighten me," Michelangelo said.

"Stop talking about shit movies! SCULPTURE is the real art! MICHELANGELO is my God! I BECAME A FUCKING ACTOR JUST BECAUSE I WAS FUCKED BY FUCKING FATE! By the way, why are you named Michelangelo? Being named is your freedom; being disgusted with your name is also my freedom!" Loonol Borrymoro left after speaking.

Michelangelo was stunned, and it took him a long time to relax. He walked ahead quickly as if fleeing from this recent embarrassment.

—

Michelangelo came to a crossroad. In the center of the crossroad was a dark, rectangular parallelepipe extending upward. The sky above was a square of pure black, and because there was no star in it, it was darker than night.

Michelangelo walked into the darkness. With a little flickering light, he saw the back of a man in a floating chair smoking a cigar—even if he could not actually see the iconic face, any fan could recognize the figure as Morlon Brondo.

Michelangelo was so nervous that he could barely move. However, he still mustered up the courage to approach him. "Hello, distinguished Mr. Brondo. I'm Michelangelo DiCaprio. Please forgive me for disturbing you. Do you have time to tell me how an actor can give an outstanding performance playing the role of God? I think you know the secret."

"Acting is a terrible profession. From the

day you were selected for this profession, it was destined that you would no longer be happy. The only thing you could do after that was waste your time and your life." After Morlon Brondo finished speaking, he put the cigar aside and closed his eyes to rest.

As the cigar's light faded away, all Michelangelo saw was a darker and darker tone of black.

CHAPTER 16

EXERCISE CABIN

After returning from Secret Skity, Michelangelo received a notice from the director. He was required to get into high-intensity strength training to create a strong image of God.

Good's Gym, floating at 360 Hampton Dr. in the seaside skytown of Venice adjacent to Los Angeles, was a cross-shaped building composed of seven huge cubes. The main business here was virtual reality fitness training.

Carrying Elizabeth's A-Star trophy on his back, Michelangelo entered the exercise cabin. The voice prompt told him that the training system would monitor his physical and psychological conditions in order to guide him to the most appropriate training.

Then, the voice started to count down, and the light in the exercise cabin dimmed.

After the countdown, Michelangelo saw bright scenery in a brand-new "Mouse Pairk" with various huge amusement pairk facilities flying in the air.

Michelangelo discovered that these huge amusement pairk facilities turned out to be cute giant animals with peculiar shapes and colors. A group of cute little angels flew over to play with them happily.

Suddenly, a giant snake appeared. Michelangelo recognized that it was the one he had met in Death Valley! The giant snake twisted its body, opened its big mouth, and swallowed all the little angels and giant animals. Suddenly, a long golden stick appeared, one end of which floated in front of Michelangelo. Michelangelo grabbed the end of the stick in both hands. He tried to swing hard, but it didn't move at all. The giant snake stretched out its red tongue and approached him. At this critical moment, Michelangelo realized that using too much or too little power would not help; only using moderate strength could make the stick emit the greatest strength—it was the system guiding him to warm-up, and this "long golden stick" was made of tactile magnetic waves which had a sense of touch and weight.

As Michelangelo, using moderate strength, hit the giant snake again and again with the golden stick, the giant snake's movements gradually became slower, until it lay motionless on the ground and finally turned into golden light and dissipated. The long golden stick also disappeared. The little angels and giant animals were rescued. They flew back into the air, making cute gestures to thank Michelangelo.

Michelangelo felt that he had done a great thing; he was in a good mood. Just then, the "mouse" he met when he first came to Mouse Pairk appeared in front of him. The "mouse" seemed a little surprised when seeing Michelangelo but quickly regained its vitality and performed an aerobic dance. Michelangelo was stunned. *It is the aerobic dance Elizabeth performed in the subway car!* After dancing for a while, the "mouse" made the same unique movements that Elizabeth had invented for Michelangelo.

"Oh my God! Are you Elizabeth? Do you know how much I worry about you? Do you know how much I miss you?" Michelangelo shouted, going to take off the "mouse's" headgear. The "mouse" protected its headgear while continuing to dance, then turned and ran.

Carrying Elizabeth's A-Star trophy on his back, Michelangelo called Elizabeth's name as he chased after the "mouse." The little angels flew low, opening their arms to block the "mouse"; however, the "mouse" avoided them easily. Then the little angels and the giant animals planted avocado trees. The trees instantly grew; they were ten times thicker and taller than ordinary avocado trees. The cube-shaped avocados on these trees were ten times larger and harder than conventional avocados. Then the little angels and the giant animals built a towering Great Wall with these avocados.

The Great Avocado Wall blocked the "mouse." Then the "mouse" started to climb it. Because the Great Avocado Wall's surface was slippery, the "mouse" almost slipped off several times. Fortunately, a few little angels held it for him. Michelangelo felt anxious. He quickly climbed the Great Avocado Wall to chase the "mouse."

The "mouse" then lost his footing. Because the incident happened suddenly, even the little angels flying nearby could not save it in time. The "mouse" fell off the Great Avocado Wall, and Michelangelo automatically jumped off the Great Avocado Wall.

In the process of falling, Michelangelo tried to catch the "mouse" but failed. The weightlessness generated by the non-tactile magnetic waves made him scream.

Suddenly, Michelangelo felt his body stop falling and he began to float upwards, drifting higher and higher. When he heard the chorus of the familiar song "Who Can Save the Poor California Kids," he felt that he had crossed the sky and floated over the Great Avocado Wall. He found a row of phantoms singing on the top of the Great Avocado Wall—they were the ghosts of those classmates who had climbed the Great Wall with him in the old days. When he approached these phantoms, they dissipated; the singing became more and more distant...

Carrying Elizabeth's A-Star trophy on his back, Michelangelo called Elizabeth's name and ran looking for her on top of the Great Avocado Wall. Eventually, he heard a voice calling his name. He ran over and found the "mouse" holding onto the edge of the top of the Great Avocado Wall with both hands. *It is indeed Elizabeth!* She was still wearing the mouse costume, but the headgear was gone. Michelangelo was surprised, but happy, and quickly pulled her up.

"Elizabeth, this is your trophy. I'm giving it back to you!" Michelangelo took the A-Star trophy from his back and assisted Elizabeth in carrying it on her back.

Suddenly, the Great Avocado Wall began to vibrate. Michelangelo and Elizabeth looked down on the earth. They saw countless coyotes rushing mightily toward the Great Avocado Wall; some of them had reached the foot of the Great Avocado Wall and started climbing.

Michelangelo began pushing the avocados down the side of the wall to stop the coyotes from attacking; Elizabeth did the same.

Michelangelo completely forgot that he was in the exercise cabin and that these "avocados" he was throwing down from the "wall" were actually tactile magnetic waves.

Michelangelo soon realized something was wrong—the more avocados they pushed down the wall, the shorter was the Great Avocado Wall and the closer were the coyotes. He hurriedly stopped Elizabeth. "If we continue to throw the avocados down, they will arrive soon!"

Elizabeth continued to push the avocados and shouted, "You are confused! If we stop throwing the avocados down the side of the wall, they will get here even sooner."

While they were arguing, an arrow was shot at them. Elizabeth automatically stood in front of Michelangelo. The arrow hit the A-Star trophy she was carrying. Elizabeth was startled and fainted right on top of the wall.

Michelangelo saw a man in armor with braided hair. When the man got closer, Michelangelo looked at his face. *It is Madd Damon!*

Meanwhile, some icons of various armors

and weapons appeared in the sky. Michelangelo clicked on an icon of a suit of armor, and then he was outfitted in heavy armor. He clicked on an icon of a glaive and then a heavy glaive appeared in his hands—the armor and the glaive were tangible magnetic waves.

Madd Damon reached the wall top. He rushed towards Michelangelo with a scythe taken from the air. Michelangelo waved the glaive, roared towards Madd Damon. Whenever Michelangelo knocked Madd Damon's weapon out of his hand, Madd Damon grabbed a new one from the air; similarly, whenever Madd Damon knocked Michelangelo's weapon out of his hand, Michelangelo picked up a new one from the air as well. They also changed different armors to ward off their opponent's various weapons and to get the most appropriate protection.

After all their weapons were used up, Michelangelo and Madd Damon fought each other with their bare hands. They gradually approached the place where Elizabeth was lying in a coma. To prevent Madd Damon from hurting her, Michelangelo tried to lead Madd Damon in the opposite direction, but he slipped on a cracked avocado and fell. Madd Damon then pounced on Michelangelo and grabbed him around the neck.

When Madd Damon opened his mouth to show Michelangelo his coyote teeth, he was suddenly knocked down—Elizabeth had woken up and hit Madd Damon on the head with her A-Star trophy.

Elizabeth and Michelangelo hugged each other tightly. At this point, Michelangelo saw Madd Damon standing in a trance behind Elizabeth. Michelangelo screamed. Without looking back, Elizabeth threw the trophy into the air.

Madd Damon pounced on the flying trophy. As the trophy fell, he howled and fell towards the earth.

—

"How can you throw away such a good thing!" The phantom flew up and waved the trophy. "You don't want to keep it? I do!" He kissed the trophy and flew away.

At this moment, Michelangelo found another "Madd Damon" rushing toward them.

Michelangelo suddenly remembered that Madd Damon had a twin brother Watt Damon. *It must be him!*

Watt Damon grabbed a fauchard and ran toward Michelangelo and Elizabeth. Michelangelo had no weapons anymore, so he had to drag Elizabeth to run. Holding the fauchard, Watt Damon went after them in hot pursuit.

At that very moment, a giant fire rose up from the ground, immediately engulfing all the running coyotes. The fire continued to rise, destroying all the coyotes that were climbing. Suddenly, Elizabeth slipped on a cracked avocado and fell. Michelangelo hurried to pull her up. Meanwhile, Watt Damon roared and charged at them again. At this most urgent moment, the fire that rose up engulfed him. Michelangelo took Elizabeth's hand and jumped off the top of the wall, just before being destroyed by the flames.

Michelangelo and Elizabeth landed in front of a guardrail. He held the guardrail, looked out, and could not help screaming, "Mom!" It turned out that he and Elizabeth were standing in the torch of the Statue of Liberty, and the face of that goddess was his own mother's face!

At that moment, Michelangelo felt the safety and warmth that he had been missing for a long time. He and Elizabeth hugged each other tightly, overlooking beautiful New York, beautiful America.

After the virtual scenes gradually disappeared, Michelangelo realized that he was still in the exercise cabin, sweaty and tearful.

—

Michelangelo followed the voice prompt and went into the relaxation cabin. Tactile magnetic waves stretched his muscles, gases of different pressures and temperatures massaged him, and the wonderful relaxing music relieved his tension—this relaxing music was not created by musicians; it was generated by the AI relaxation system based on his psychological and physiological data. To protect human music creativity and the music industry's rights, this music was only permitted to be used in the areas of rehabilitation and treatment, and it was not permitted to be performed and published as entertainment products.

The training session was over. Although Michelangelo was exhausted, he looked forward to the next training. He was also a little nervous—he did not know what kind of thrilling experience the system would design for him in the following training because he could not know many aspects of himself nearly as well as the system could.

CHAPTER 17

ACTING LESSON

On this day, at Good's Gym, Michelangelo came to the nutrition room after training and relaxing. He held out a finger and drew a circle above a circular object embedded in the ground. The circular object rose and turned upside down to become a floating sofa. After Michelangelo sat down, it began to detect his physical condition. After a while, a cup of a nutritious shake, made according to his physical condition, flew toward him on an unmanned aerial vehicle. After Michelangelo picked up the cup, and the aerial vehicle flew away.

When the scheduled time was up, a straw

popped out, and a sweet voice reminded him to drink. The inside of this cup was layered. Each nutritious layer of the shake was different, so the scheduled opening time was also different.

Michelangelo finished the first layer of the nutritious shake. *Tastes great!* While waiting for the next layer to open, he looked around boredly and found the famous, strong veteran action star Airhold Skywarzenegger. Although Michelangelo and Airhold Skywarzenegger did not communicate much before, they often met at movie events. Michelangelo had to step forward to greet him. "Mr. Skywarzenegger, it's nice to meet you!"

"Oh, the superstar is here. How's it going? Did you have a good workout?" Airhold Skywarzenegger said.

"Don't laugh at me. You are a real superstar, especially in the gym!" Michelangelo said. "To be honest, it's cool to work out here! I regret that I didn't follow your example to exercise earlier!"

"Hahaha." Airhold Skywarzenegger was obviously in a good mood. "Speaking of gyms, I built up my muscles here. I have a deep relationship with this gym!"

"Then Mr. Sirtallone's muscles were also developed here?" After Michelangelo finished speaking, he immediately felt that he had said something wrong. *It may be inappropriate to mention a famous action star to another one.*

"I'm sure not because I've never met him in this gym! His muscles seemed to be a bit big, but their contours were stupid. He always played silly big guys whose faces never crack a smile. Maybe he was limited by the muscles he developed during his body-building experience," Airhold Skywarzenegger said. "The muscle contours built through the workouts in this gym come with a deep sense of wisdom, making me suitable for both strong and smart character roles! Of course, I have the ideal muscle contours because I am lucky enough to have chosen the right gym!"

Michelangelo did not know how to answer. After all, Skylivebester Sirtallone's muscles seemed to him to be perfect.

"My God, is there a children's pairk?" A loud voice was heard. Michelangelo and Airhold Skywarzenegger looked in the direction of the voice and found Skylivebester Sirtallone talking and laughing with companions. "I have never figured out why that man's muscle contours are so delicate, and now I have the answer! This is a place for little girls! There are all kinds of thoughtful physical protection and psychological care offered here. Is this a place to train a little princess?" Skylivebester Sirtallone turned around and found Airhold Skywarzenegger and Michelangelo looking at him. His expression instantly turned into one of indisputable kindness and honesty. "Hi, bro! Today is my lucky day! I meet the king of action movies!" Skylivebester Sirtallone walked quickly towards Airhold Skywarzenegger. "This place is awesome! I envy you for spotting this place so soon! No wonder your movies are always wonderful! You chose the right gym!"

"Dude!" Airhold Skywarzenegger affectionately hammered Skylivebester Sirtallone in his chest. "You are a real hero! Your natural fitness method is really amazing! You dared to jump to the ground to race and fight with beasts. It was a much better show of bravery and strength than we show here facing only virtual figures! You were the only one who dared to do this in California! So I love your movie! I am a big fan!"

Michelangelo stood beside them and tried his best to squeeze a smile. No matter how hard he tried, the smile was still a bit distorted, not as credible as theirs were.

"That was all in the past; now I am old, and I am not so flexible. If I jump to the ground now, it will be equivalent to delivering fast food to the animals," Skylivebester Sirtallone said, laughing with Airhold Skywarzenegger.

"Hey, man, are we unable to keep up with the times? Or are the times going backward? Why are some action actors nowadays like that?" Airhold Skywarzenegger said to Skylivebester Sirtallone.

"Yeah, the authentic muscular style is lost. How did the current action star get his muscles? How can they be so smooth and delicate? Looking at his chest, I almost thought he was a female star!" Skylivebester Sirtallone said.

"You are right! We were thinking the same thing! You are talking about that kid!" Airhold Skywarzenegger said. "Let's keep his name out of it and save face for this young guy! However, I don't understand why he always grinned in such a silly way at the camera? What kind of movie was he starring in? An action movie or a comedic movie?"

"My bro," Skylivebester Sirtallone said, "don't be angry with the young man! Who hasn't been young? Who hasn't been stupid? We should understand him!"

"Hahahaha." A burst of loud laughter was heard. Airhold Skywarzenegger, Skylivebester Sirtallone, and Michelangelo followed the voice and realized that it was the action actor Diwayone Joysun just implicitly mentioned by Airhold Skywarzenegger and Skylivebester Sirtallone. While walking along showing off his huge, muscular body, Diwayone Joysun was grinning and talking excitedly with his companions. "I can't stand those old guys. Were they in extreme pain during their training? Otherwise, how could they have developed their facial expressions to look like that? It seemed that the whole world owed them avocados. What kind of movies were they starring in? Action movies or debt collection movies?"

Michelangelo noticed that Airhold Skywarzenegger and Skylivebester Sirtallone looked at Diwayone Joysun with a neutral expression. The so-called "neutral expression" was an expression that could be changed at will. According to the situation, no matter what expression was needed next, this one was reasonable.

After finding Airhold Skywarzenegger and Skylivebester Sirtallone here, Diwayone Joysun's face instantly resembled a blooming flower. "My God, how lucky I am! I meet two seniors at the same time! Two action movie legends! You two heroes are still so strong, and your muscles are still great! When I reach your age, I will be content to have half of your muscles!"

"The young people nowadays are nice! They are talented and polite!" Airhold Skywarzenegger said to Skylivebester Sirtallone. "This kid has great muscles!"

"I can't agree more!" Skylivebester Sirtallone said. "It seems that we don't have to worry about the future of action movies at all. How great young people are! With young people like this, action movies will become stronger and stronger!"

In this happy and cordial atmosphere, Michelangelo finished drinking all the layers of his nutritious shake. He bid farewell to these three action stars, entered the bathing cabin, and took a comfortable gas bath.

—

When Michelangelo got dressed and walked out of Good's Gym, it was almost dark, and Good's Plaza was bright.

"How was the lesson today?" a voice said. *It was Mr. Brondo's voice!*

Michelangelo turned around and found an "old lady" in a fancy dress sitting in a floating armchair and smoking a cigar.

"Mr. Brondo! I'm so glad to see you here!" Yes, no matter how Morlon Brondo was dressed, Michelangelo could recognize this figure.

"Did you learn anything?" Morlon Brondo waved his hand, and a floating armchair rose from the ground.

Michelangelo thanked him and sat next to him. "Mr. Brondo, why did you leave Secret Skity? Isn't it going to cause trouble?"

"The law does not permit the secret people to reveal their identity, but it does not prohibit us from leaving the Secret Skity," Morlon Brondo said. "It is not difficult for actors—acting in different characters is our profession."

"So, do other secret people often go out as well?" Michelangelo asked.

"Yes, I'm the laziest about going out. Female stars prefer to do this—they can't stop shopping," Morlon Brondo said. "Did you learn anything from this acting lesson?"

"Acting lesson?" Michelangelo asked.

"It was," Morlon Brondo said. "How was the performance of those three guys just now? Did they teach you a good lesson?"

"Ah, indeed, their performances were amazing!" Michelangelo said.

"These three guys have reached a high professional level in performance; they even perform in their everyday lives. They are all good actors," Morlon Brondo said, taking an item from his bag and handing it to Michelangelo. Michelangelo took it. It was an A-Star Award trophy!

"The essence of acting has always been in this trophy. It is a pity that most people only pay attention to the glorious gold of the trophy but ignore its shape," Morlon Brondo sighed.

Michelangelo looked at the trophy. "The shape of this trophy is a hedgehog and a deer. I always thought it was just a decoration. Is there any deep meaning in it?"

"Everything in the world is a combination of contradictions. In everyone's heart, there exist the sharpness of hedgehogs and the gentleness of deers. Everyone needs to constantly change themselves in response to the many contradictions in life and to adapt to the multiple aspects of things. Only by expressing the dynamic change in this contradiction can it be called 'performance,'" Morlon Brondo said, taking the trophy back from Michelangelo and putting it back in the bag. He made a gesture, and a garbage collection unmanned aerial vehicle flew over.

"It's a bit heavy; there is no need to keep it," Morlon Brondo dropped the bag containing the trophy into the aerial vehicle, waved his hand, and the aerial vehicle flew away.

Morlon Brondo took a long pull at his cigar and said, "I'm tired. I want to go back." He called a fried egg car and flew away.

Michelangelo waved goodbye and then stood there, recalling what the master just said.

—

After a while, the fried egg car flew back. The hatch was opened, and Morlon Brondo poked his head out. "By the way, young man, would you tell me your name again?"

"My name is Michelangelo DiCaprio, Mr. Brondo," Michelangelo replied.

"Oh, okay, thanks. Nothing, I just can't remember the password to open the door." Morlon Brondo closed the hatch and flew away.

CHAPTER 18

SKYQUAKE

Michelangelo was deeply entangled in his predicament. He was obsessed with how to act the part of God well enough to win the A-Star Award. However, he also worried that if he won the award, he would be listed in the "list of immortals" and lose the opportunity of experiencing death. He believed that death could liberate his soul, allowing him to cross the Great Wall and return to the United States to reunite with Elizabeth and his mother.

However, after the movie *Back to the Dust* started being shot, the intense work temporarily got his mind off his entanglement in this difficult situation.

—

According to the director's plan, the last scene was going to be the most shocking scene in California movie history—restoring the magnificent scenes of the Sistine Chapel Ceiling created by Michelangelo di Lodovico Buonarroti Simoni, the great Italian Renaissance artist, into the REAL SKY! Although post-production technology could be used to generate this scene, the director thought that the virtual images lacked vitality and could not achieve the visual shock he hoped they would. Therefore, he used California's latest remote organism magnetic levitation technology to accurately send the actors to the designated position in the sky, which caused the movie's budget to break a historical record. However, the movie studio's AI actuarial system was certain that if the movie studio used the material from this shooting in surrounding projects, it would be profitable. The system calculated a demonstration plan, suggesting constructing a roofless chapel ten times larger than the Sistine Chapel. The dynamic 3D hologram of real people would be permanently projected in the sky above the chapel. Visitors entering the chapel would view the extraordinary spectacle against the real sky. This plan resulted in the entire movie studio being drowned in cheers because FAME FOREVER is every creator's ultimate dream.

—

Because this shooting event had become the most significant social hotspot in California, almost all the fried egg cars in California were requisitioned. Even a vehicle shortage warning was triggered, causing the AI Transportation System to produce spare fried egg cars. The AI Security System blocked curious people from entering the shooting scene. However, because the shooting scene was in the real sky, the system could not stop them from watching from a distance in fried egg cars. As a result, California had the most bizarre sight in its history: In the air outside the restricted area, there were countless fried egg cars floating in layers. These cars seemed to form an oversized cylinder, densely surrounding the shooting area. Because the AI Transportation System had a default setting that showed this situation was impossible, it did not have a solution to deal with this situation.

The movie studio was helpless and happy with this situation. This kind of spectacle of spectators watching a shooting scene nationwide was unprecedented in California's history, which meant that this movie's popularity would be unparalleled.

—

Under the staff's guidance, Michelangelo, dressed as a bearded God, began to do warm-up exercises to make his muscles reach the best condition. It was a wonderful moment for an actor to participate in such a magnificent shooting of a movie.

Michelangelo found Madd Damon also arrived at the shooting scene. He was also doing warm-up exercises—he was invited to play the part of Adam. Judging from the state of his excitement, he must have thought that he was playing a part as the protagonist in the movie.

Many stars had also come as guest actors, including some former A-star Award for Best Actor winners. Airhold Skywarzenegger, Skylivebester Sirtallone, and Diwayone Joysun were among them—the Sistine Chapel Ceiling was full of strong characters, and many of them were suitable for the three of them.

Because the scene that would be shot was very complicated, hundreds of working groups had undergone repeated tests before shooting.

—

"ACTION!" the director yelled. Hundreds of unmanned aerial movie cameras floating at different locations started to work. The remote organism magnetic levitation equipment made Michelangelo fly in the air like God. A group of actors behind him performed, imitating the prototype in the Sistine Chapel Ceiling. "God," played by Michelangelo, slowly flew towards "Adam," played by Madd Damon. Michelangelo stretched out his right arm and pointed his index finger at Madd Damon. Madd Damon, who was lying reclining on a hillside setting, propped up his naked body with his right arm and extended his left arm.

When the fingertips of "God" and "Adam" collided, a dazzling light exploded.

The sky shook violently! The earth was used to experiencing numerous earthquakes, but it was a "SKYQUAKE" this time.

Meanwhile, all the magnetic equipment in California failed. All objects which floated by magnetic energy—including buildings, roads, vehicles—either fell to the ground, rushed into the sky, or collided. Some actors were thrown to higher positions in the air; some were thrown to the ground crying. Layers of fried egg cars were like fragments from a large cylinder that disintegrated instantly, scattered in all directions.

Michelangelo tried to catch a child actor next to him. He failed because he was falling upwards—yes, Michelangelo experienced for the first time that "falling" could also be upwards.

In the process of falling upward, Michelangelo felt time slowing down. He opened his eyes and found that the clouds resembled the scene of "The Creation of Adam" in the Sistine Chapel Ceiling. The sunshine passed through the clouds, making this scene sacred.

As the bearded image of God made up of clouds became clearer, Michelangelo discovered that this image was actually a face with three eyes wearing an aerospace helmet! To be precise, it was not the face of a human being—this face was exactly the same as the alien face that often appeared in movies. God's right arm reaching out to Adam was actually a tentacle protruding from the alien's forehead!

The clouds that resembled the shape of the hillside where Adam was gradually changed, becoming more like a plump female figure. The outline of her torso was evident, and her breasts and vulva were vivid. At this moment, Michelangelo found Madd Damon crying and falling up into the clouds in the shape of the female body. The place where he fell was the position of the "womb" of the "woman!"

It turned out that "Adam" in the Sistine Chapel Ceiling was a metaphor for a fetus in the womb of a pregnant woman! The great scene in "The Creation of Adam," by Michelangelo di Lodovico Buonarroti Simoni, which had always been looked up to by generation after generation, actually depicted A THREE-EYED ALIEN FROM A SPACESHIP REACHING OUT A TENTACLE FROM HIS FOREHEAD TO A FETUS IN THE WOMB OF A PREGNANT WOMAN.

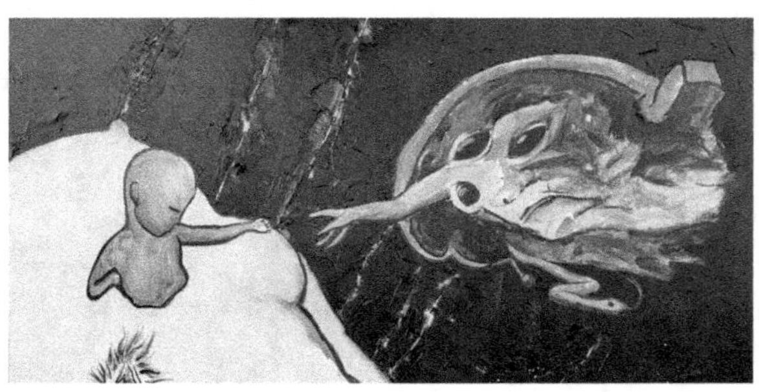

Oh my God! What am I seeing? In great shock, Michelangelo DiCaprio felt that he was flying through thick dark walls, and he found Elizabeth and his mother waving to him in the far light...

(End of Volume One)

MARK HARRIS (Author)

Novelist
Illusion Artist
Chinese Homophones Writer
Chinese Full-Rhymes Writer
Chinese Alliterations Writer
Member of the Authors Guild

He is from China and now lives in Los Angeles.
His Chinese name is transliterated as Yemen Chen. However, his pen name is Mark Harris, which is taken from the name of the protagonist of the first beloved Chinese American TV series, *Man From Atlantis.*

MAJOR WORKS OF LITERATURE
Michelangelo DiCaprio
Book of Chinese Homophones
Book of Chinese Full-Rhymes
Book of Chinese Alliterations

MAJOR WORKS OF ILLUSION ART
The Creation (2020)
The Friars (2020)

The Hedgehog and the Deer (2016)
The Bloody Night (2016)

ACHIEVEMENTS
Originator of "full-rhyme article"
Originator of "alliteration article"
Originator of "same-root homophone article"
Originator of "same-tone same-root homophone article"
Writer of the most homophone articles in the world
Writer of the most full-rhyme articles in the world
Writer of the most alliteration articles in the world
Discoverer of natural friar relief in Friar Hill

RECORDS
The first "full-rhyme article" in the world
The first "alliteration article" in the world
The first "same-root homophone article" in the world
The first "same-tone same-root homophone article" in the world
The first homophones collection in the world
The first full-rhymes collection in the world
The first alliterations collection in the world
The most homophones in the world up to now
The most full-rhymes in the world up to now
The most alliterations in the world up to now
The most tongue twisters in the world up to now

PUBLICATION
Michelangelo DiCaprio, Vol. 1: The Best Actor (2021) Los Angeles: Losget Press.
Mark Harris's Arts of Illusion: A Different Vision (2021) Los Angeles: Losget Press.
Book of Chinese Homophones (2019) Los Angeles: Losget Press.
Book of Chinese Full-Rhymes (2019) Los Angeles: Losget Press.
Book of Chinese Alliterations (2019) Los Angeles: Losget Press.
The Words of Yemen Chen (2018) Los Angeles: Losget Press.
Ballads of China (2002) Haikou: Hainan Publishing House.
Paper Tiger (2002) Haikou: Hainan Publishing House.

ELLEN BITTERMAN (Editor)

Ellen Bitterman is an editor with exceptional talent. Her English background includes teaching Writing in the New York State University System at the College at New Paltz and at Ulster County Community College. Her education includes a T.E.S.O.L. master's degree in English and an MSW, a master's degree of social work. Since 2018, Ellen has been the professional editor/proofreader in Brooklyn, New York, participated in the editing or proofreading of more than 80 fiction, nonfiction and academic documents. She also writes professional and promotional copy for authors, medical writers and commercial organization.

Through her more than 30 years of teaching writing, syntax and grammar, Ellen has cultivated a proficient set. She has contributed much to her students of composition, culminating in two works: Addison Wesley Longman's *ESL Workbook* to Accompany the Anson and Schweglers' *Handbook for Writers and Readers* and ESL Chapters for Addison Wesley *Longman's Handbook for Writers and Readers*, Published Fall 1996.

Ellen Bitterman is an editor and writing teacher. Her love of the written word as well as her delight in studying and understanding grammar systems – she speaks French and Spanish – all contribute to the dedication and affinity she has for her editing work.

Font Description

Thanks Google Open Fonts!

Amiri:
https://fonts.google.com/?query=Amiri

OpenSansCondensed:
https://fonts.google.com/specimen/Open+Sans+Condensed?query=Steve+Matteson

Wallpoet:
https://fonts.google.com/specimen/Wallpoet

Rye:
https://fonts.google.com/specimen/Rye?query=Rye

Frijole:
https://fonts.google.com/specimen/Frijole?query=Frijole

Mrs Sheppards:
https://fonts.google.com/specimen/Mrs+Sheppards?query=mrs+she#standard-styles

Online Bookselling and Reading

Paperback

United States:
https://www.amazon.com/dp/1951364104

United Kingdom:
https://www.amazon.co.uk/dp/1951364104

Germany:
https://www.amazon.de/dp/1951364104

France:
https://www.amazon.fr/dp/1951364104

Spain:
https://www.amazon.es/dp/1951364104

Italy:
https://www.amazon.it/dp/1951364104

Japan:
https://www.amazon.co.jp/dp/1951364104

Canada:
https://www.amazon.ca/dp/1951364104

Australia:
https://www.amazon.com.au/dp/1951364104

Kindle eBook

United States:
https://www.amazon.com/dp/B0969K27YK

United Kingdom:
https://www.amazon.co.uk/dp/B0969K27YK

Germany:
https://www.amazon.de/dp/B0969K27YK

France:
https://www.amazon.fr/dp/B0969K27YK

Spain:
https://www.amazon.es/dp/B0969K27YK

Italy:
https://www.amazon.it/dp/B0969K27YK

Netherlands:
https://www.amazon.nl/dp/B0969K27YK

Japan:
https://www.amazon.co.jp/dp/B0969K27YK

Brazil:
https://www.amazon.com.br/dp/B0969K27YK

Canada:
https://www.amazon.ca/dp/B0969K27YK

Mexico:
https://www.amazon.com.mx/dp/B0969K27YK

Australia:
https://www.amazon.com.au/dp/B0969K27YK

India:
https://www.amazon.in/dp/B0969K27YK

Unlimited reading on Kindle Unlimited!

https://www.amazon.com/kindle-dbs/hz/subscribe/ku?shoppingPortalEnabled=true

Published in the United States by Losget Press, Los Angeles.

Originally published in paperback in the United States by Losget Press, in 2021.

Library of Congress Cataloging-in-Publication Data

Names: Harris, Mark, author.

Title: Michelangelo DiCaprio: The Best Actor/ Mark Harris.

Description: First edition. | Los Angeles: Losget Press, 2021.

Identifiers: LCCN: 2020923991 | ISBN-13: 978-1-951364-10-6 | ISBN-10: 1-951364-10-4 | Ebook ISBN-13: 978-1-951364-06-9 | Ebook ISBN-10: 1-951364-06-6

Book design by Mark Harris, adapted for ebook

Cover design: Mark Harris

www.losget.com

E-mail: contact@losget.com

First printing. 2021.

www.ingramcontent.com/pod-product-compliance
Lightning Source LLC
Chambersburg PA
CBHW071243130626
46556CB00003B/1143

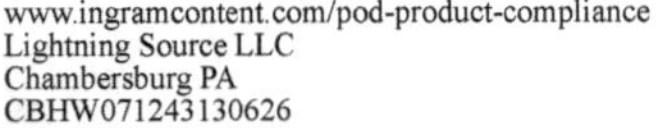

* 9 7 8 1 9 5 1 3 6 4 1 0 6 *